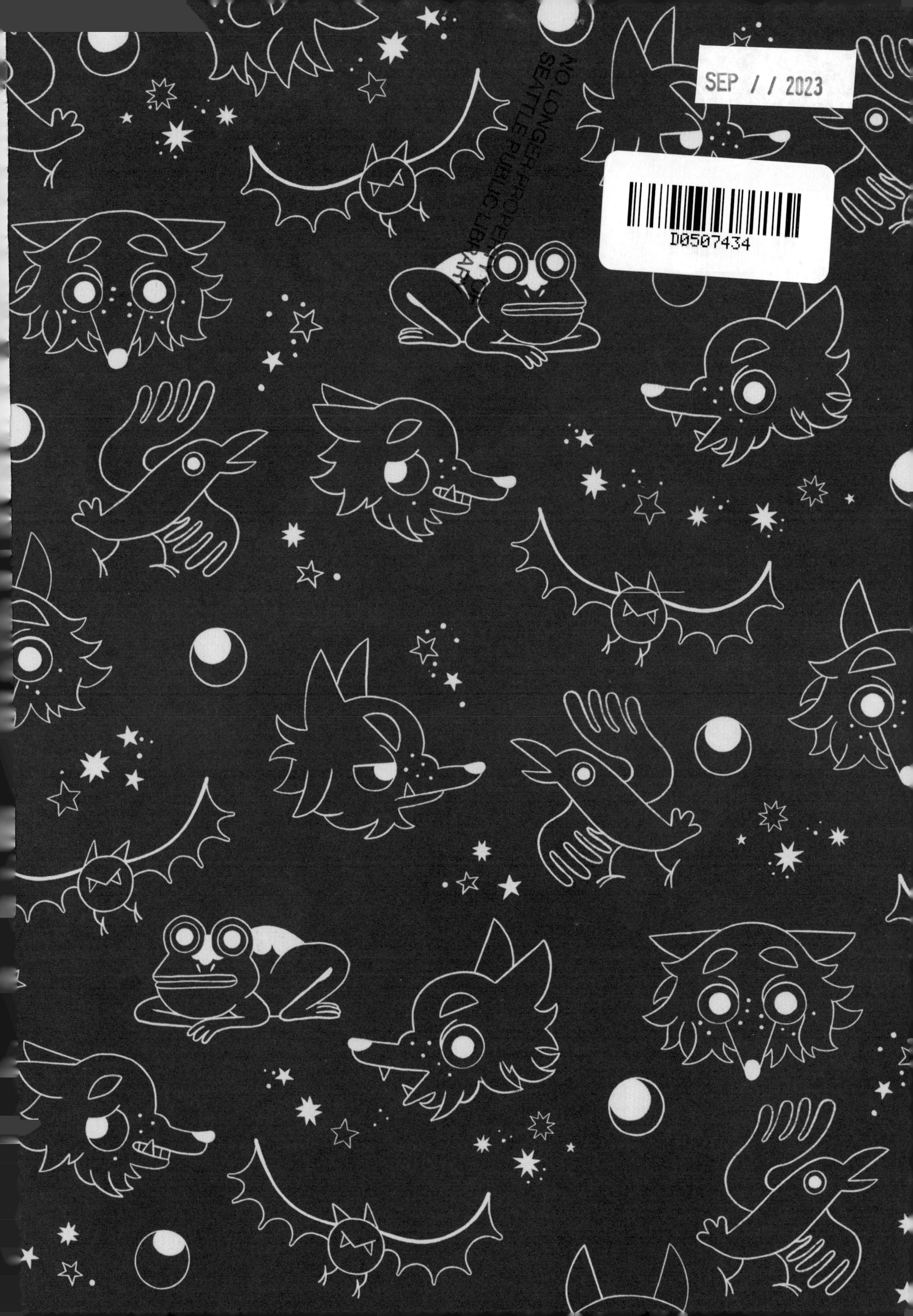

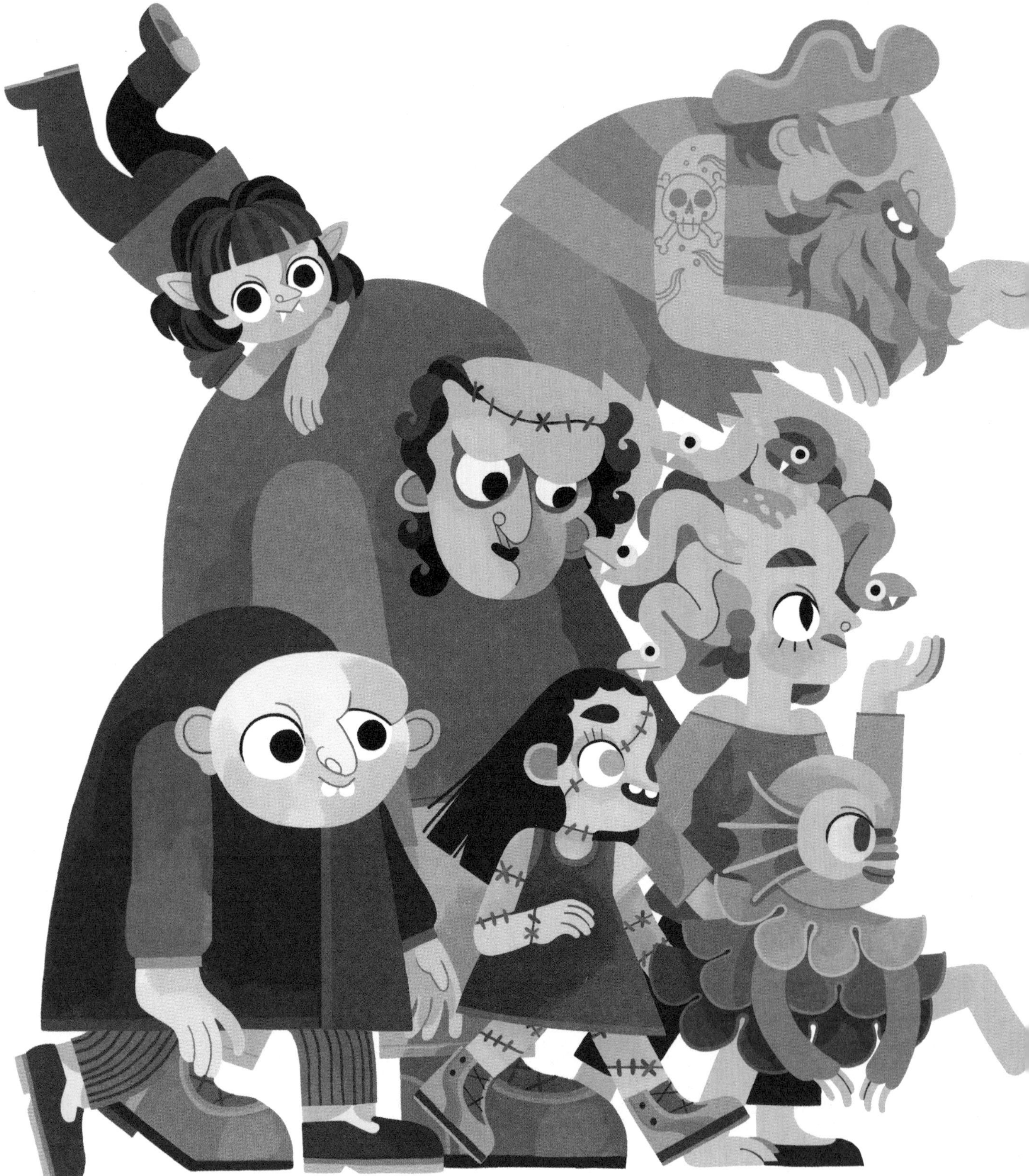

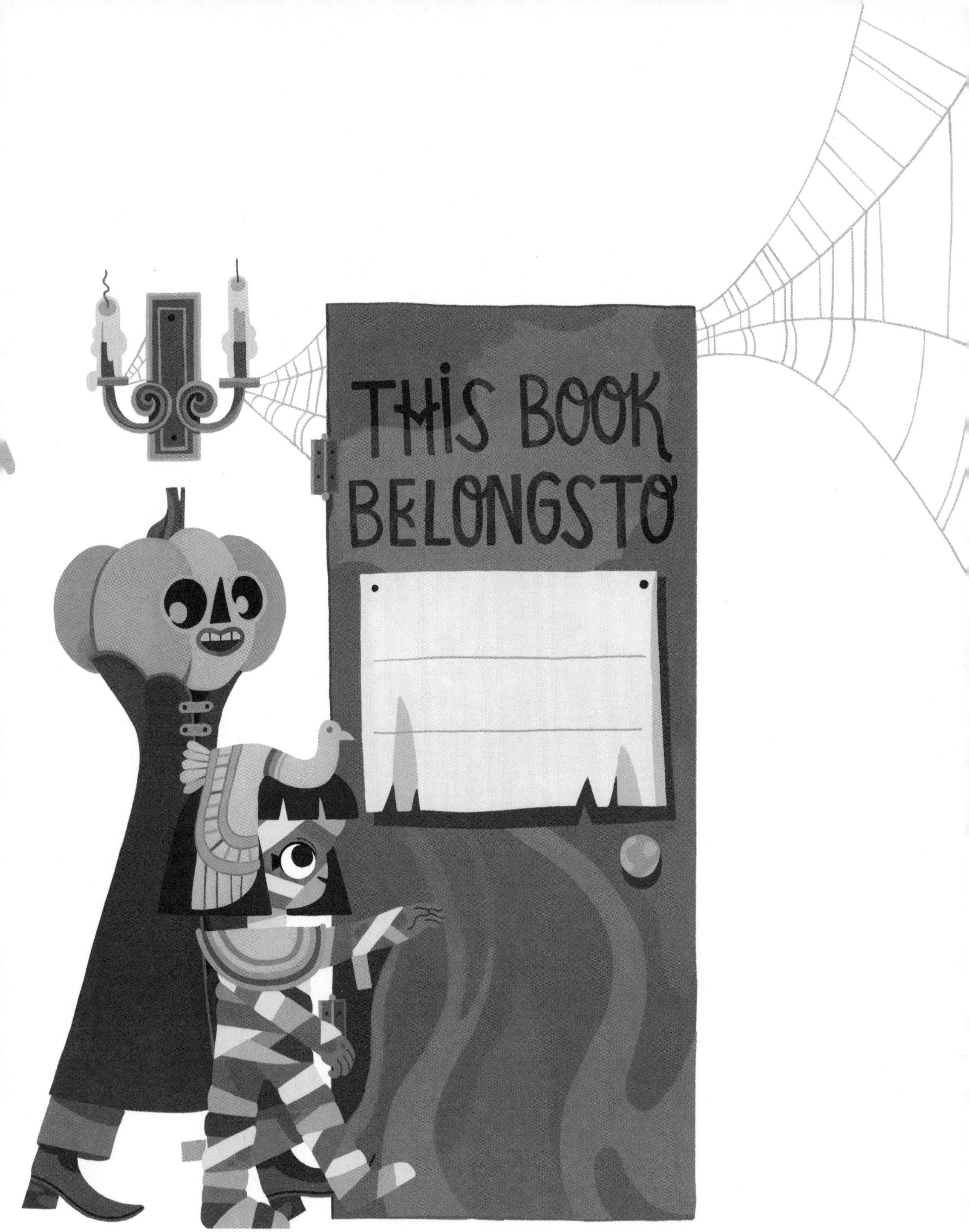
THIS BOOK
BELONGS TO

Beneath the village of Dreadbury, an unusual meeting was about to begin.

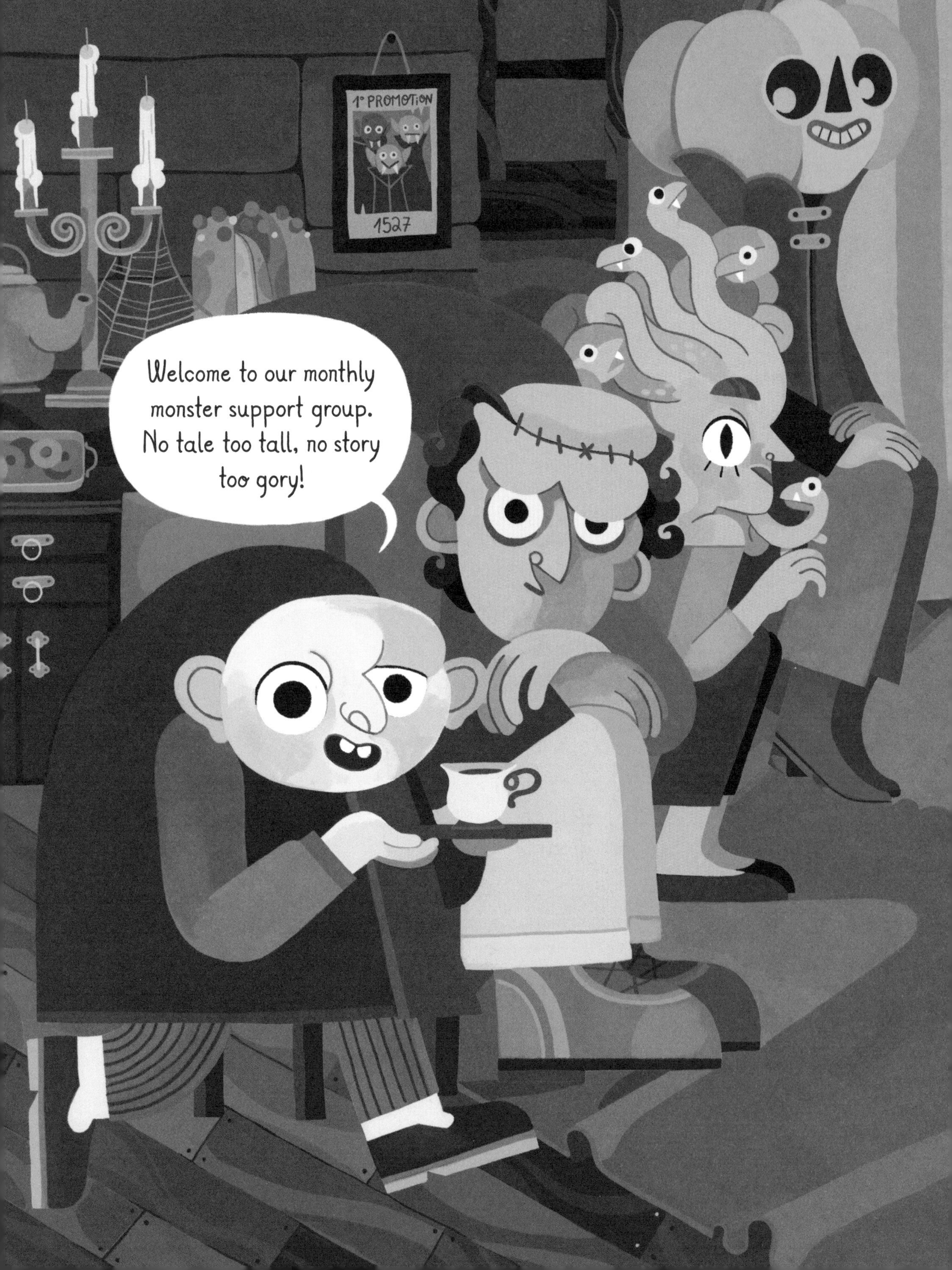
1° PROMOTiON
1527
Welcome to our monthly monster support group. No tale too tall, no story too gory!

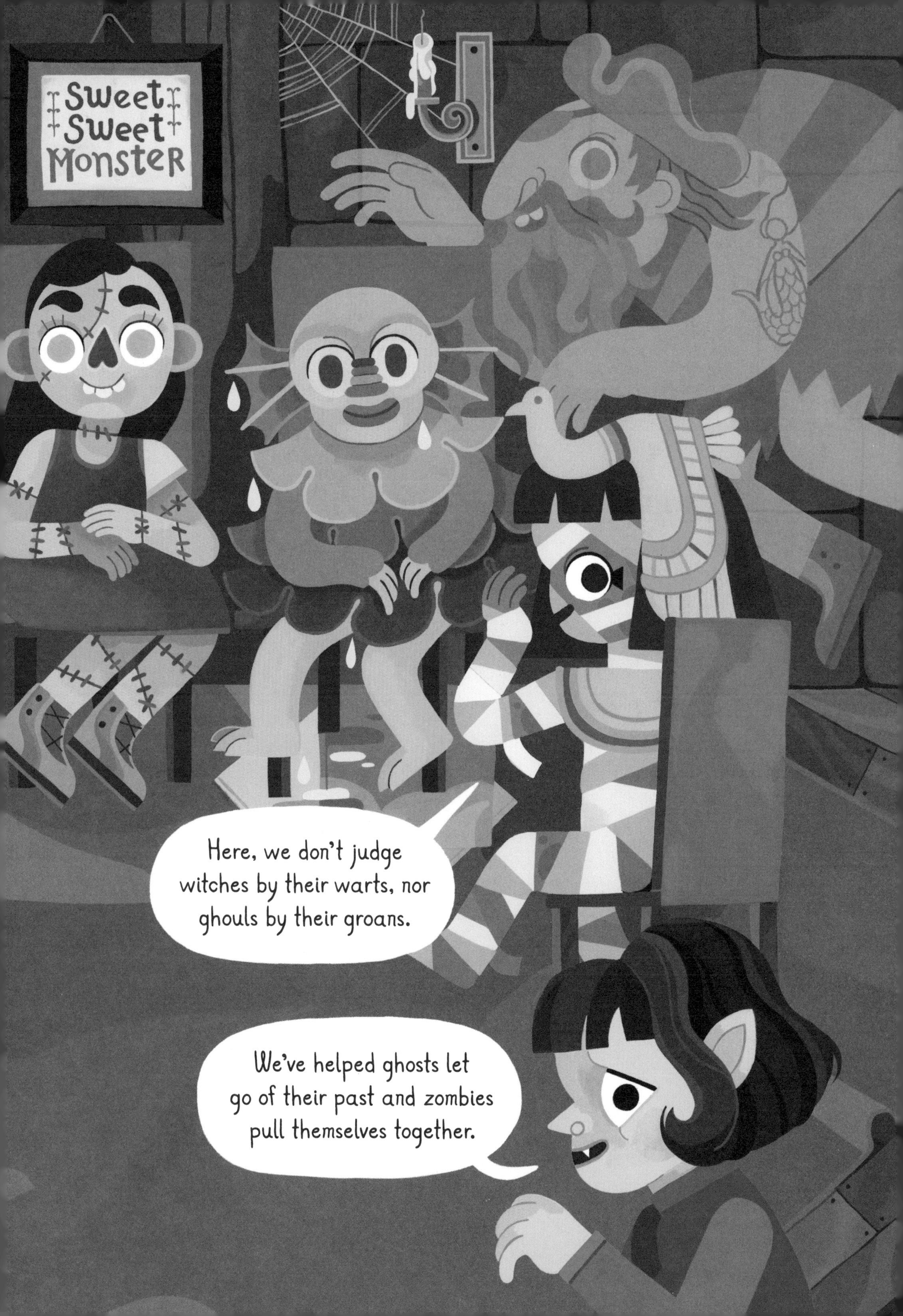
Sweet Sweet Monster
Here, we don't judge witches by their warts, nor ghouls by their groans.
We've helped ghosts let go of their past and zombies pull themselves together.

To Sabela,
my perfect little bun.

This edition published in 2023 by Flying Eye Books Ltd.
27 Westgate Street, London, E8 3RL

Concept and illustrations © Laura Suárez

Text written by Emily Hibbs

Edited by Susannah Shane
Designed by Ivanna Khomyak

1 3 5 7 9 10 8 6 4 2

Published in the US by Flying Eye Books Ltd.
Printed in Poland on FSC® certified paper.

ISBN: 978-1-83874-089-4

MIX
Paper from
responsible sources
FSC® C163799
FSC
www.fsc.org

Order from www.flyingeyebooks.com

Laura Suárez

MONSTER SUPPORT GROUP

THE WEREWOLF'S TALE

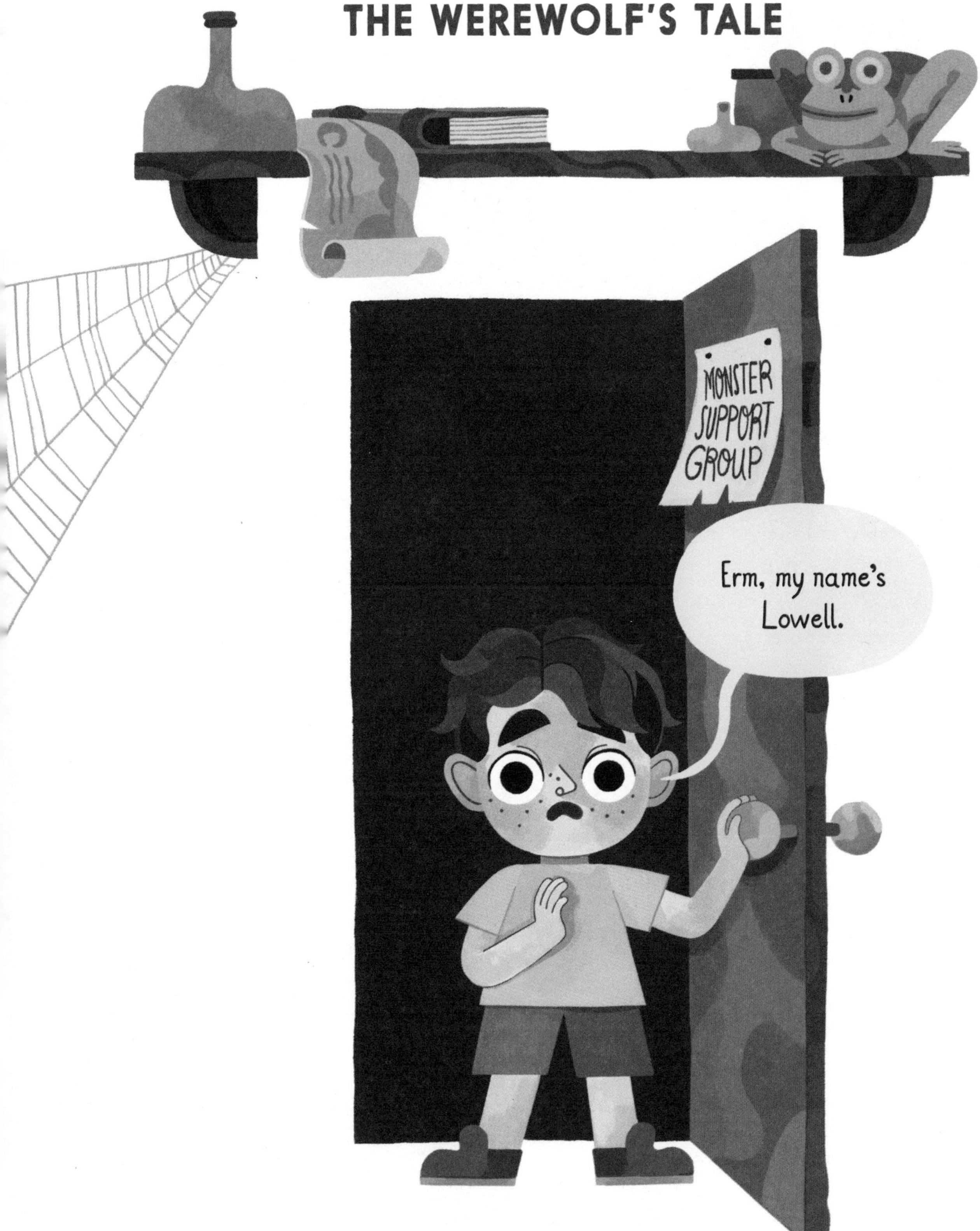
MONSTER SUPPORT GROUP
Erm, my name's Lowell.

Flying Eye Books

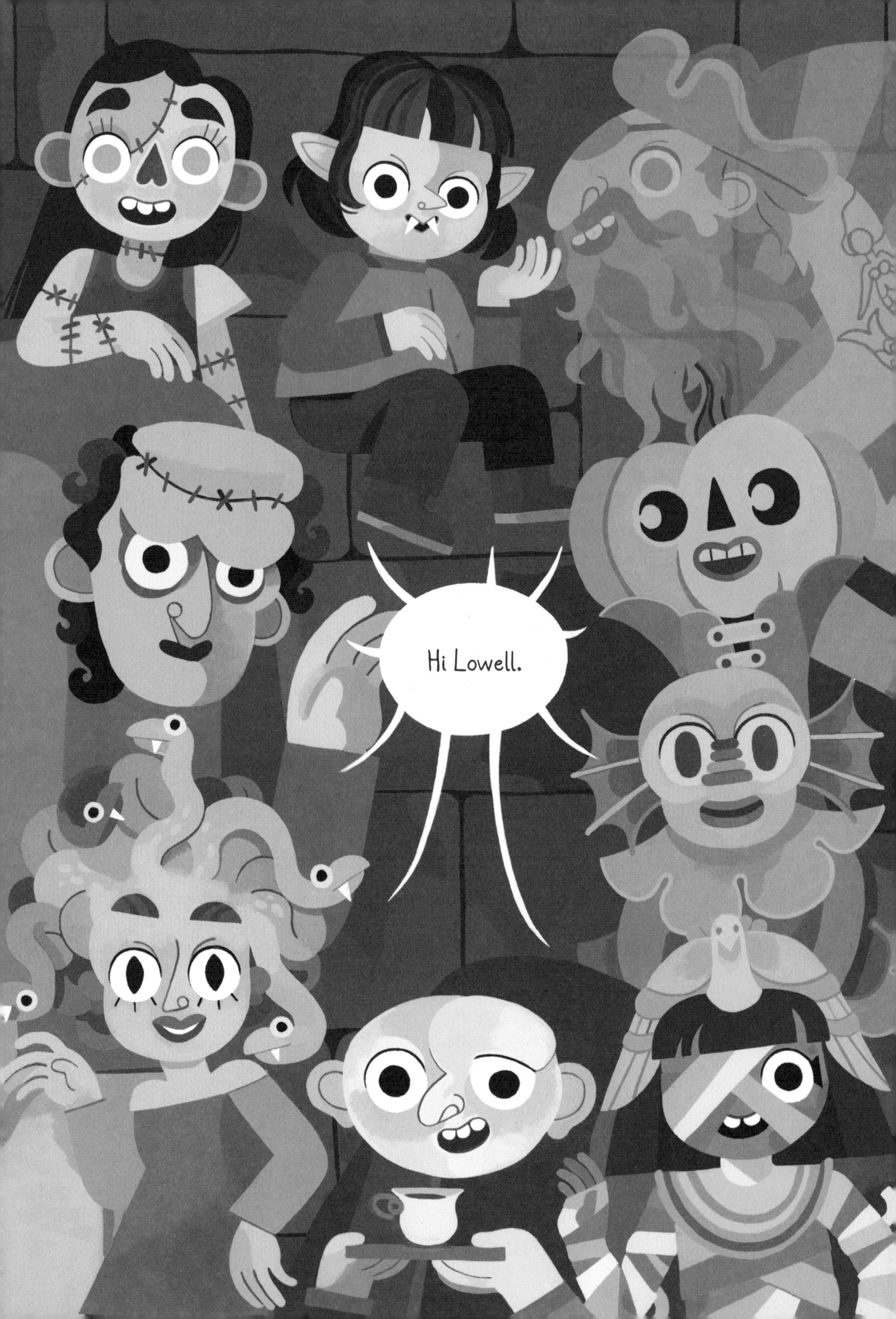
Hi Lowell.

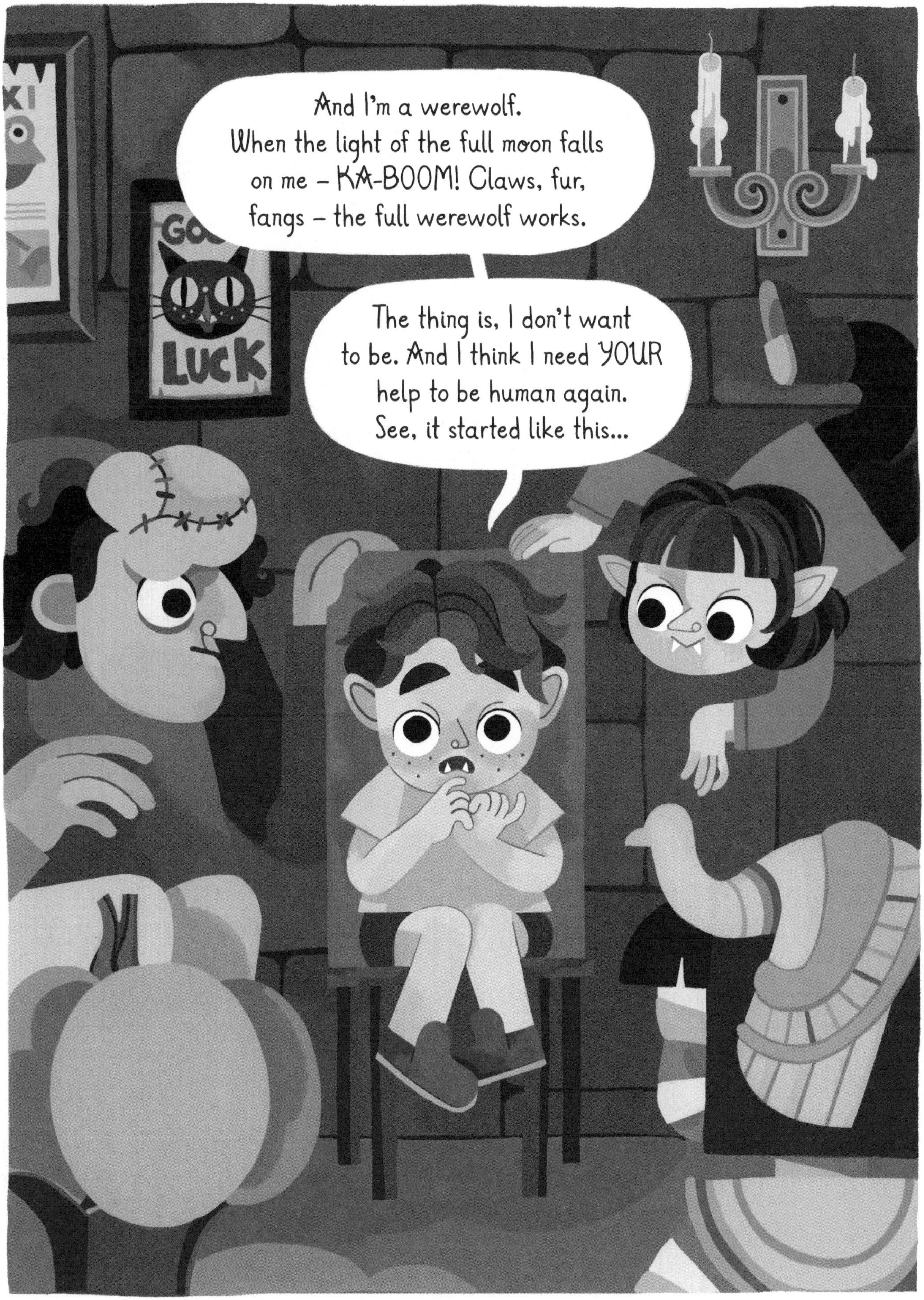
And I'm a werewolf. When the light of the full moon falls on me – KA-BOOM! Claws, fur, fangs – the full werewolf works.
The thing is, I don't want to be. And I think I need YOUR help to be human again. See, it started like this...
GOOD LUCK

So Lowell began to tell his tale.

Once upon a time, his life was normal. Lowell wasn't some mad scientist's son, or witch's apprentice, or anyone at all really.

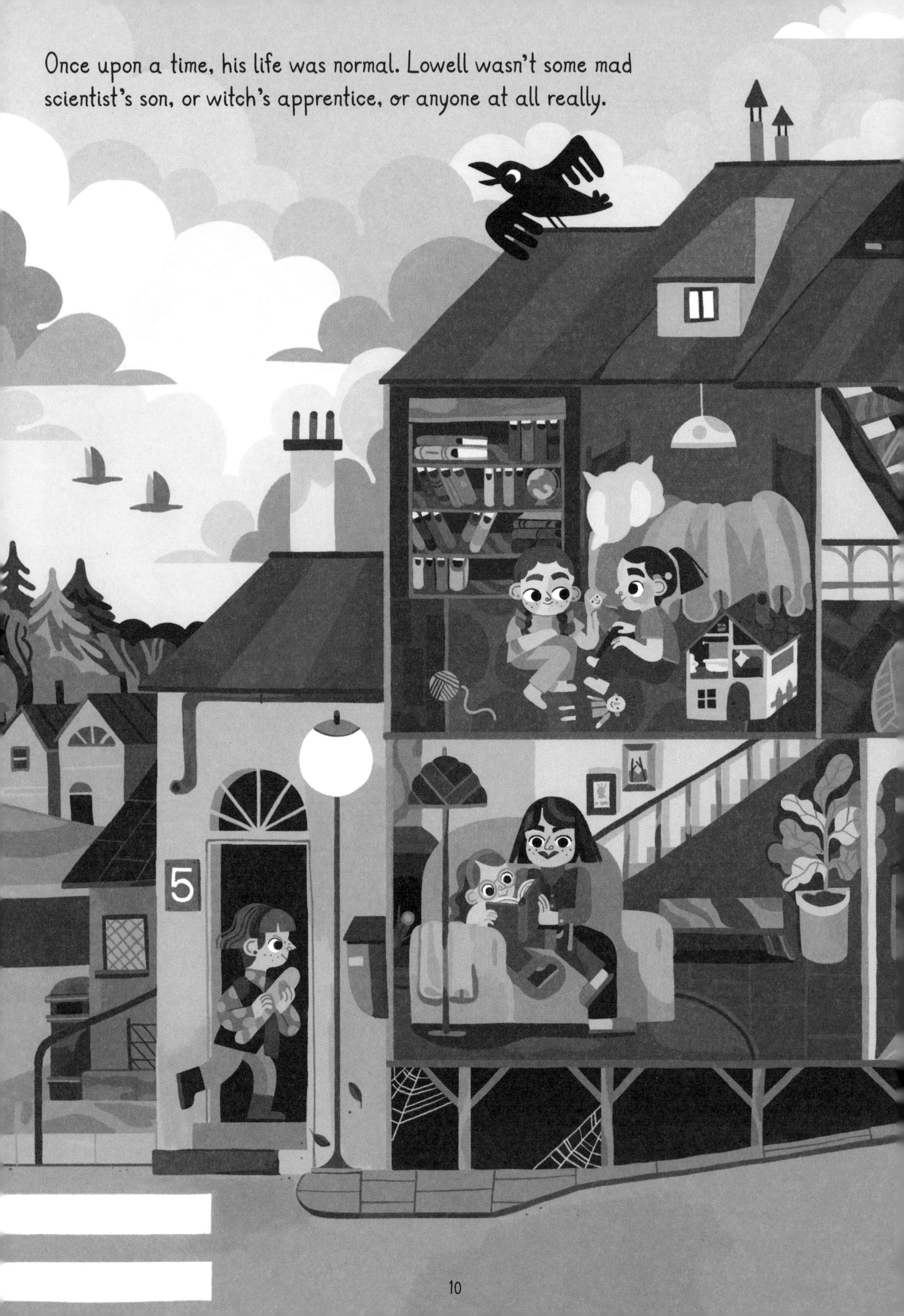
5

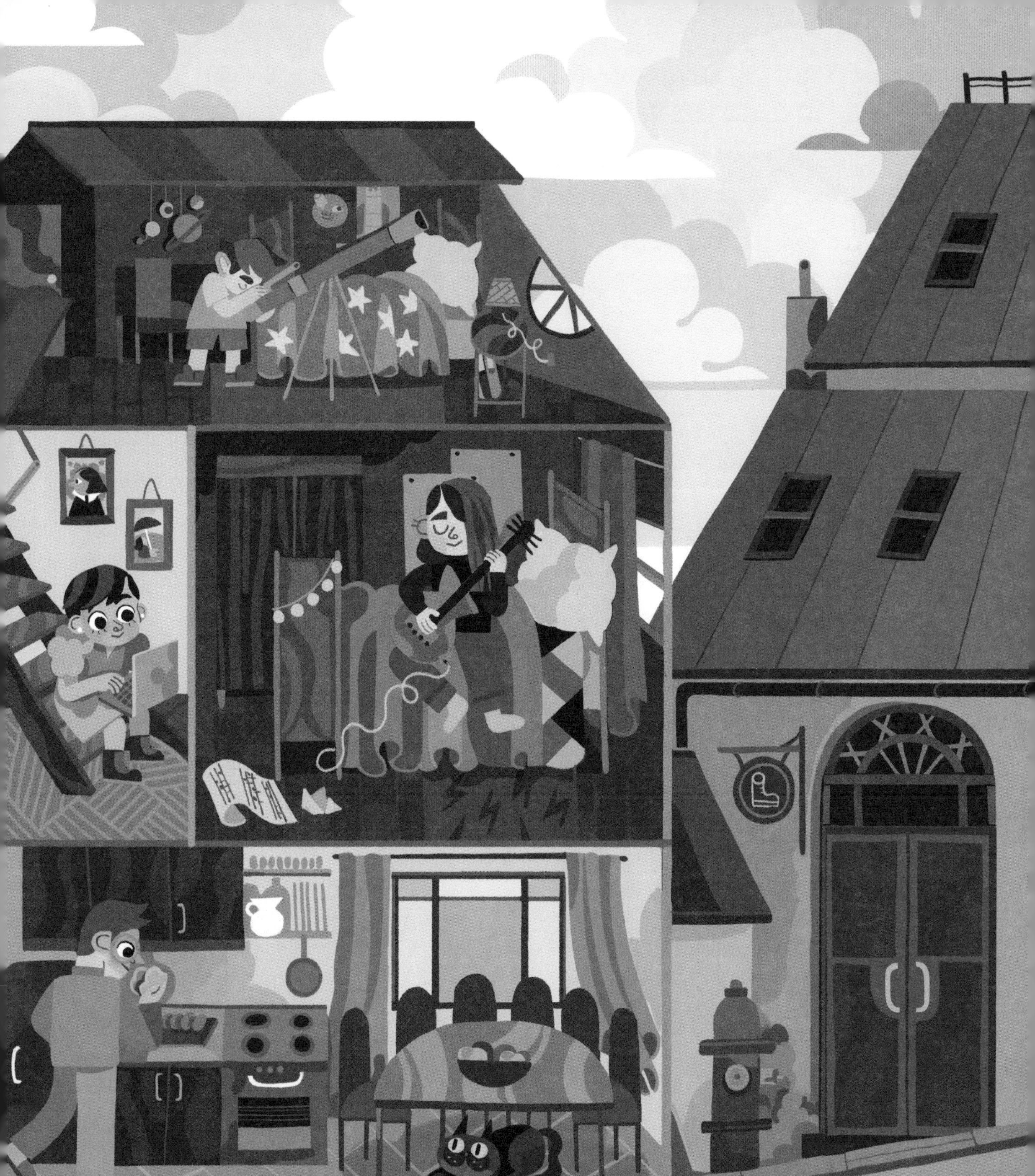

He lived on the edge of a big city with his Ma, Pa and five older sisters. Well, six older sisters if you count his twin, Lys. She was born seven minutes and sixteen seconds before him.

Then Ma got a new job, his family moved to this strange village and he had to start at a new school. That's when the trouble really began.

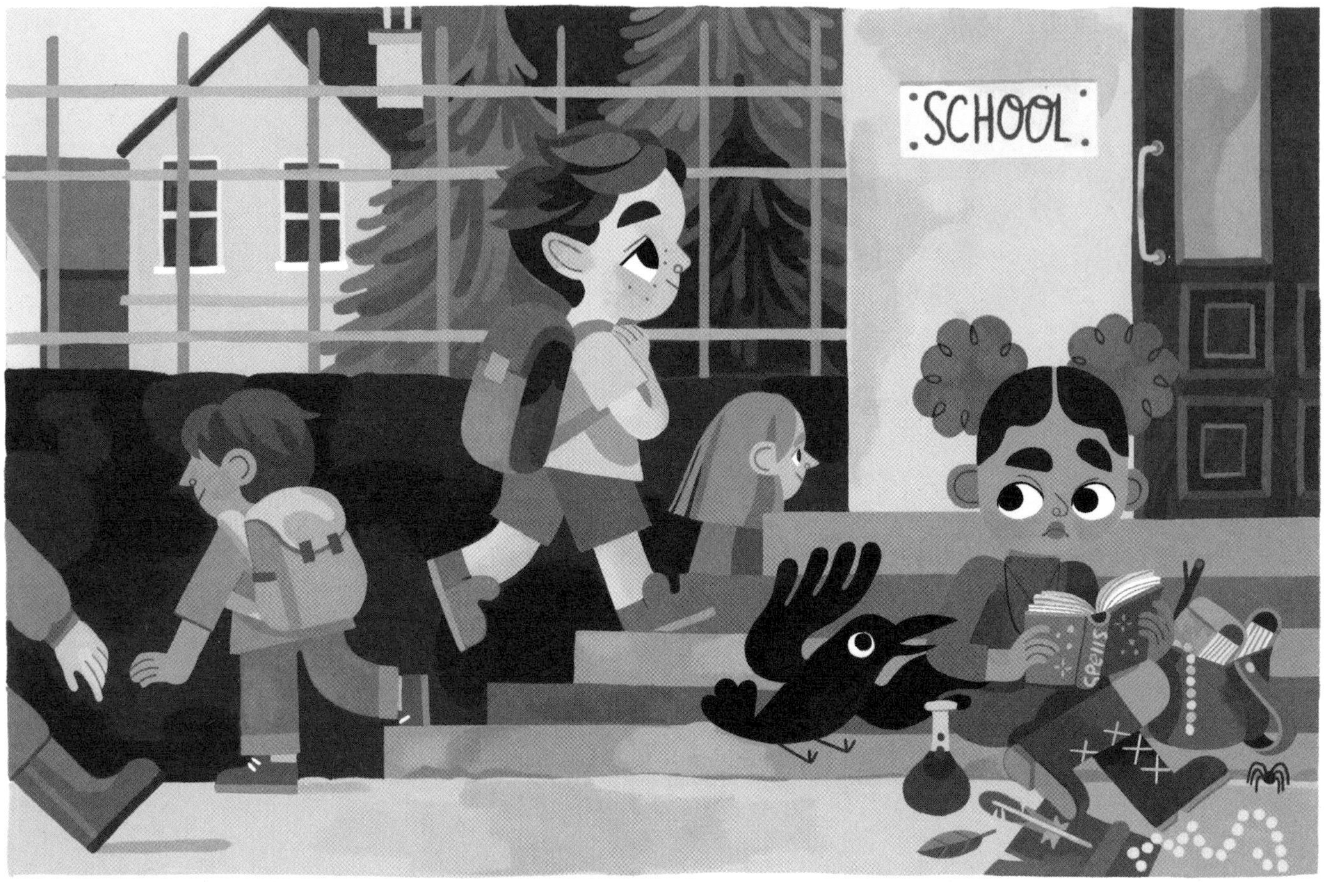
SCHOOL
Spells

Cassius Steel and his cronies decided they weren't fans of Lowell.

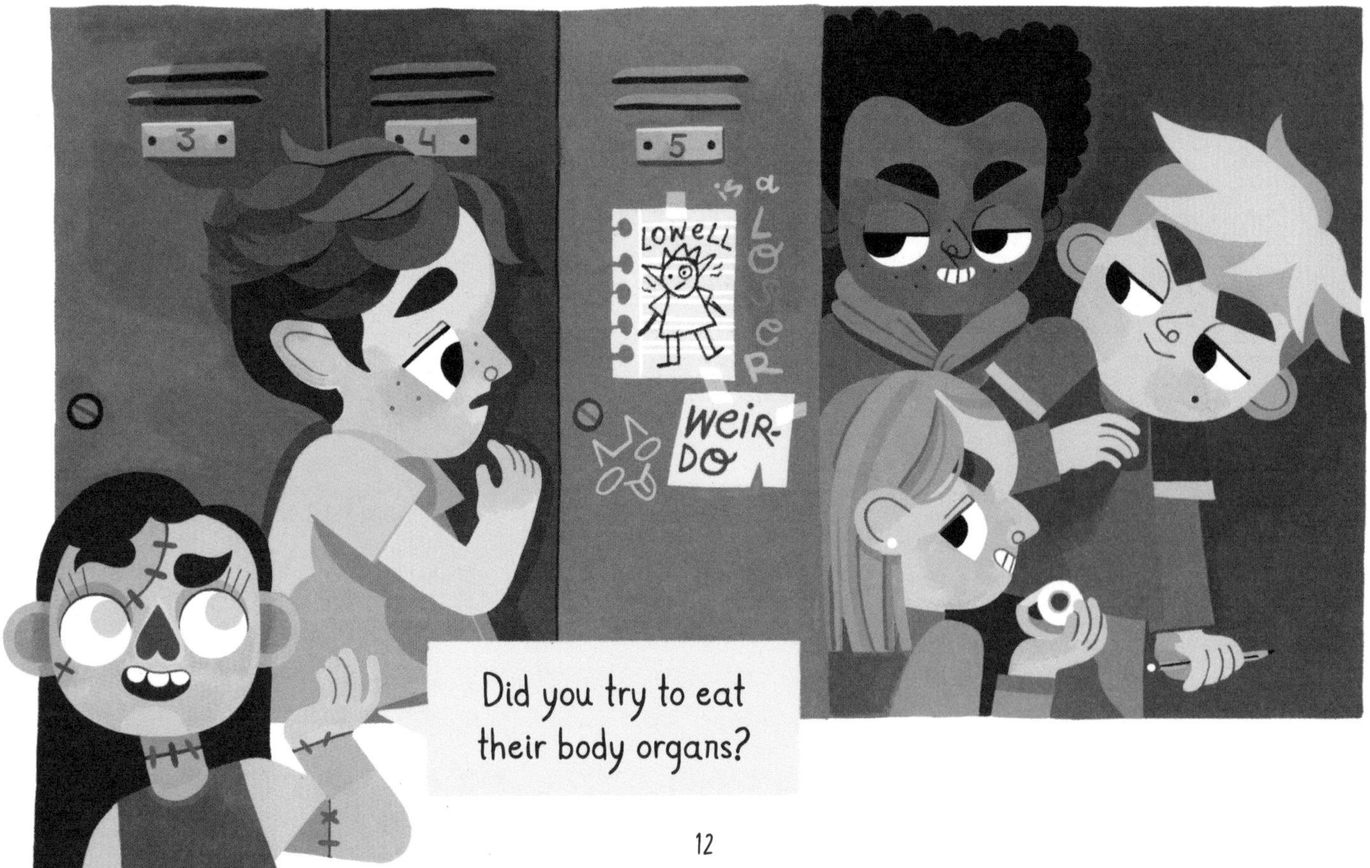
3
4
5
LOWELL
is a LOSER
WEIR-DO
Did you try to eat their body organs?

Lowell sometimes put his hand up in lessons, he didn't wear the same clothes as everyone else.

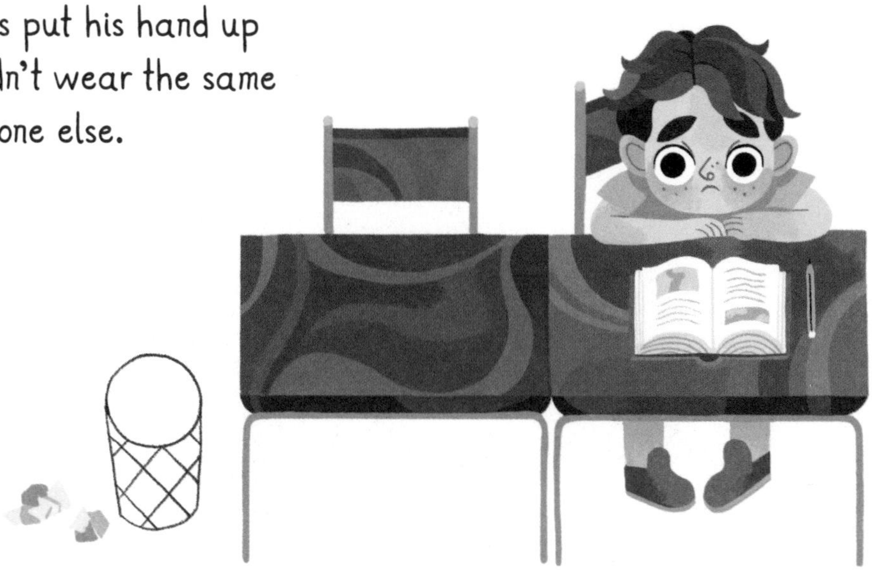

And he'd rather stare at the stars than at a screen. Maybe that made him weird in their eyes.

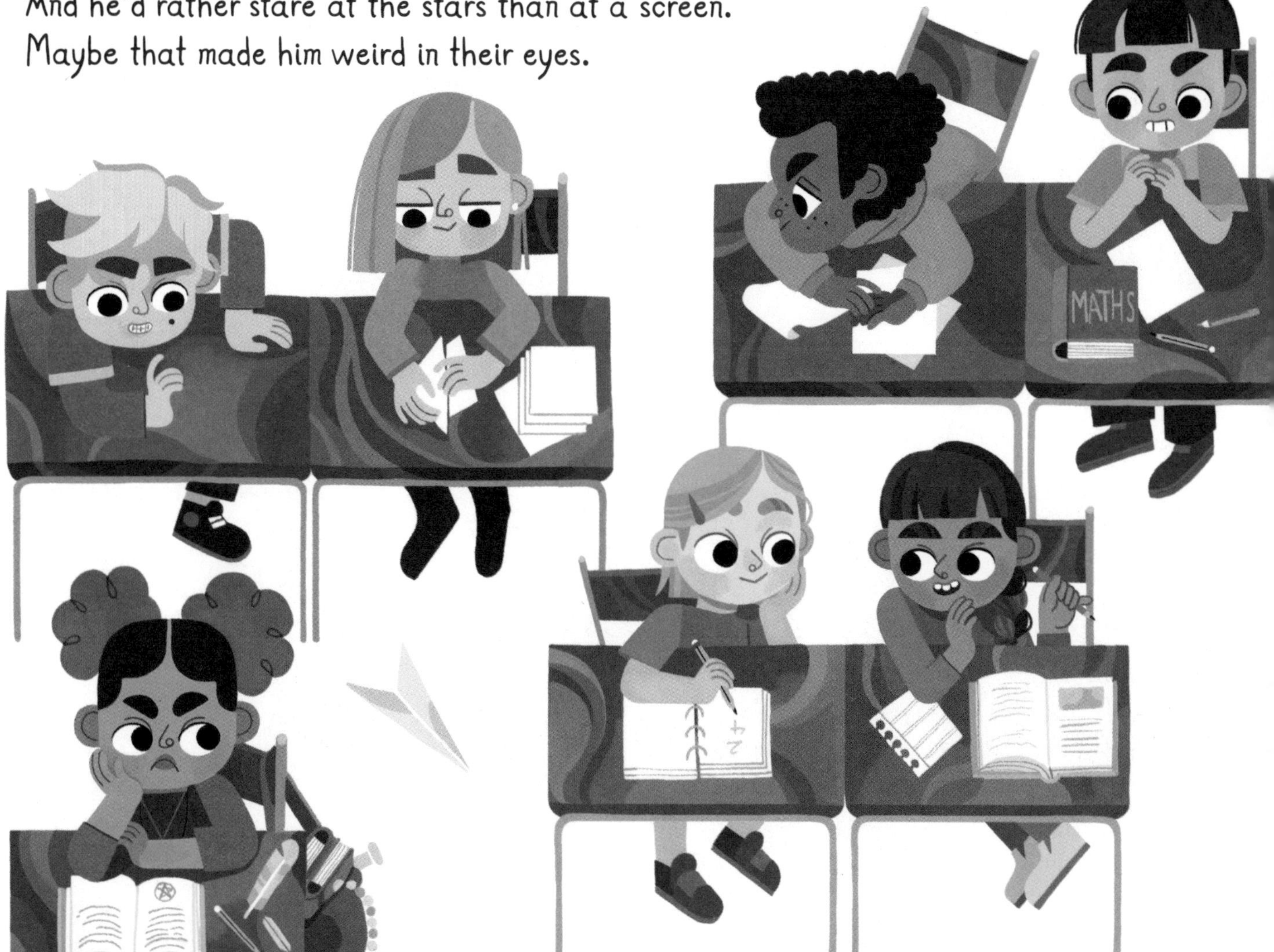
MATHS

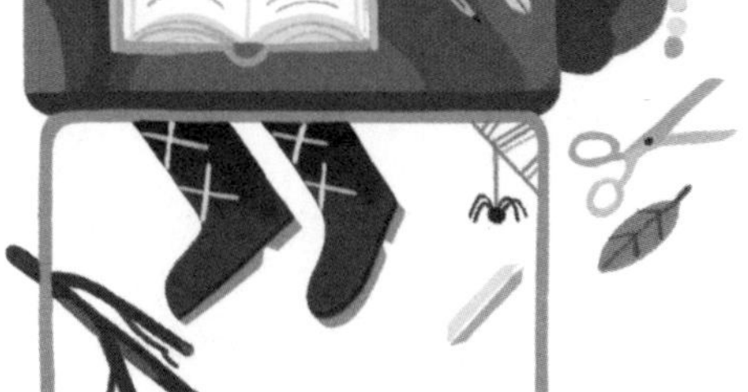

Not as weird as this girl in his class called Marie, though. Gross things are always falling out of her pockets and she crops up in the strangest places.

Anyway, things were already pretty bad: then the changes started.
To begin with, Lowell thought they were *those* kind of changes, you know?
The ones which everyone goes through to grow up.

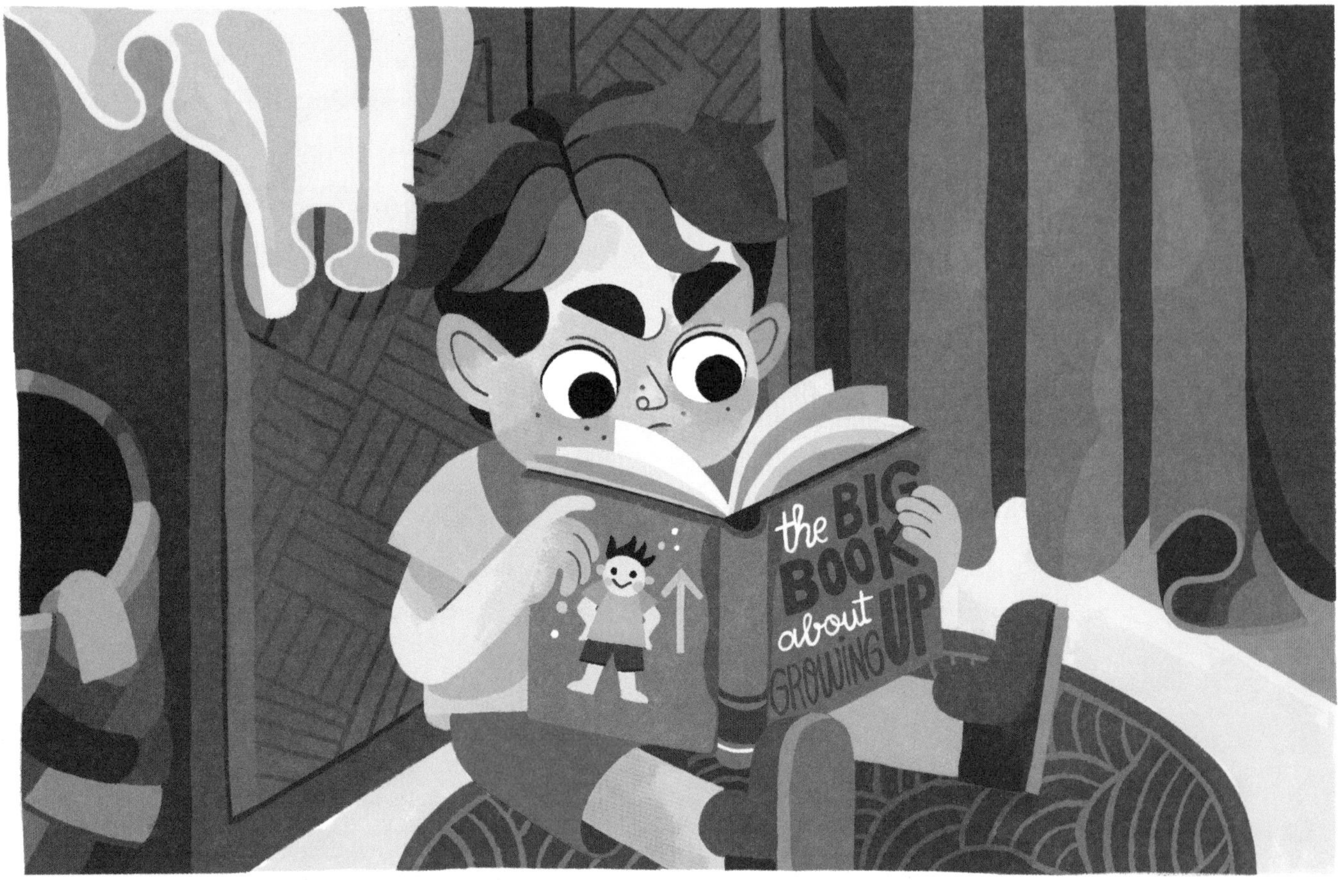
the BIG BOOK about GROWING UP

He knew that becoming a teenager made you moodier, and hairier and smellier.

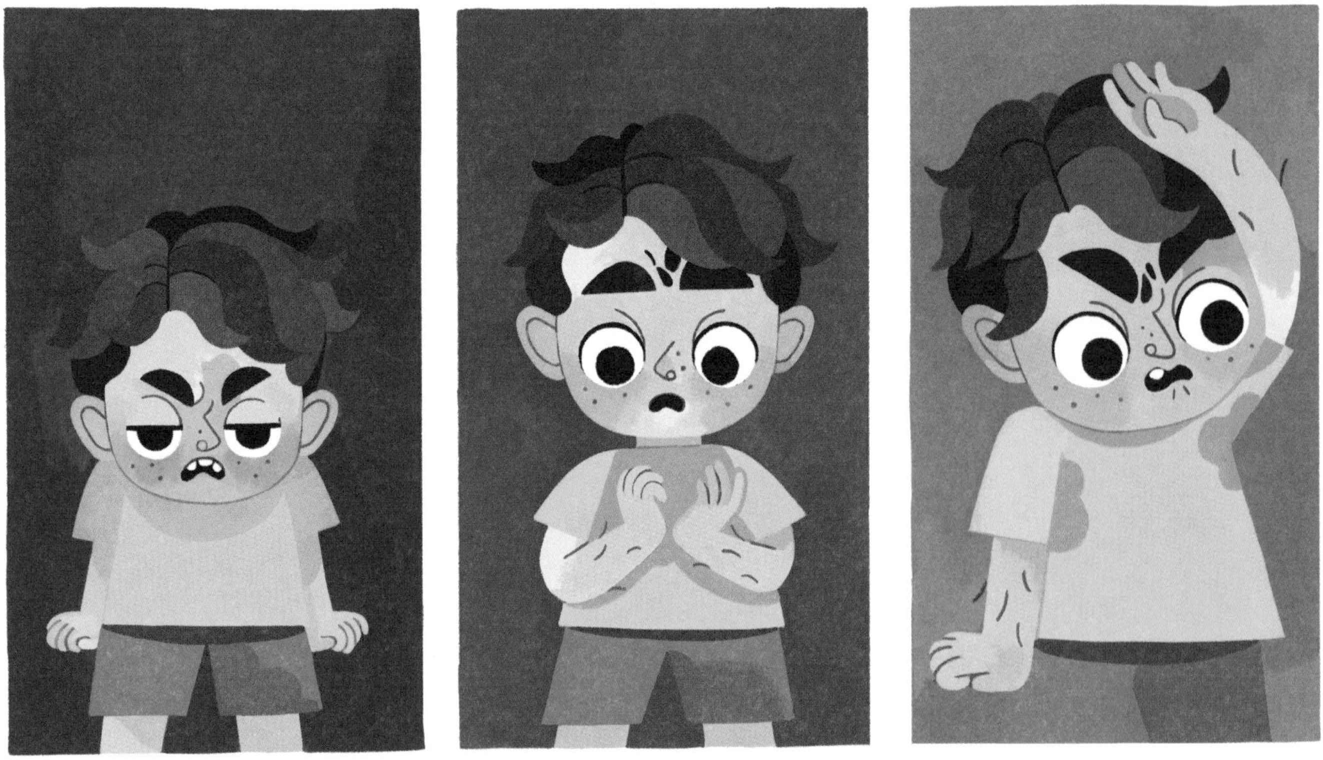

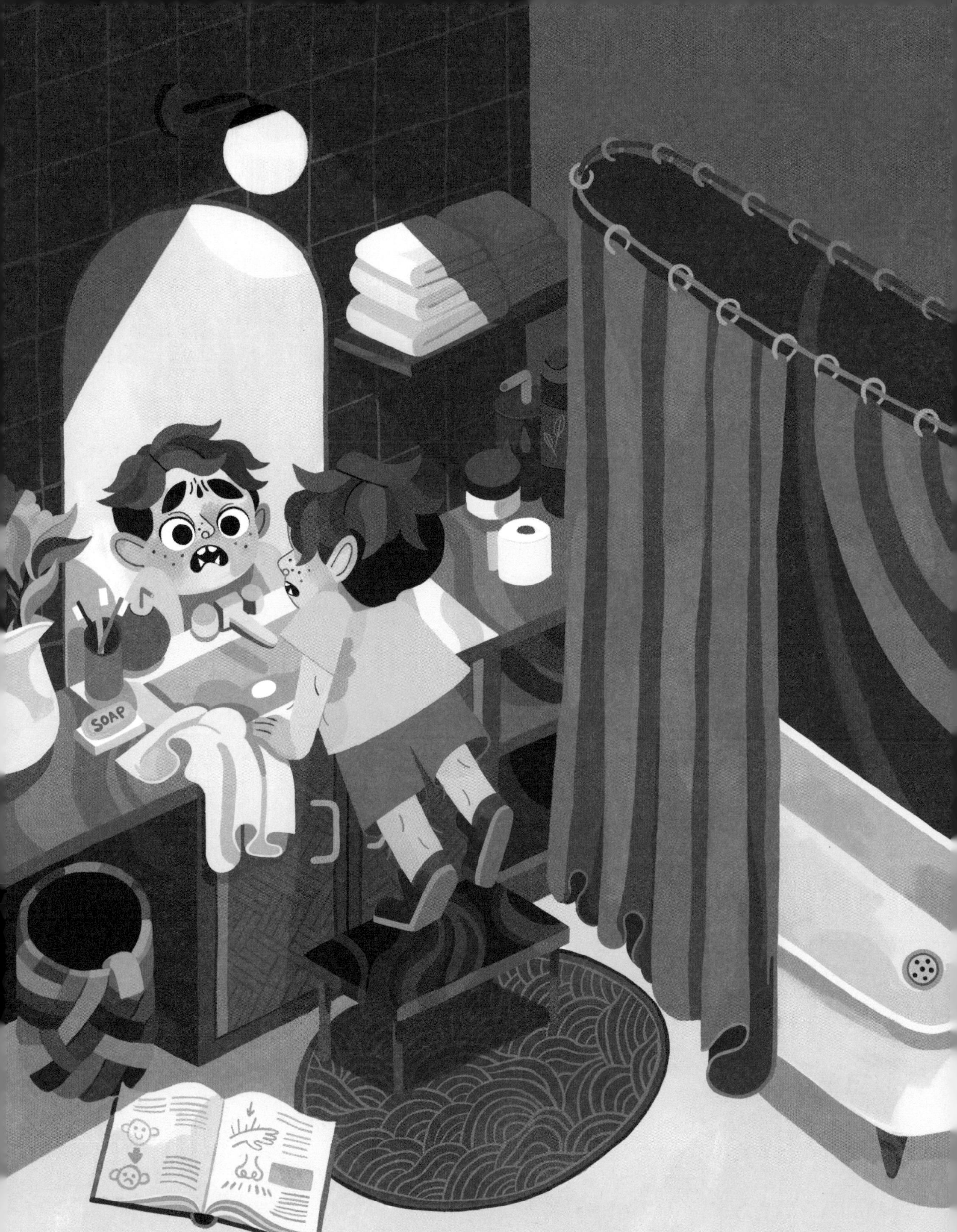
SOAP

So far, so normal, until the stranger changes. He tried to hide them, but they just kept coming back.

One afternoon, Cassius and his cronies chased Lowell all the way back from school.

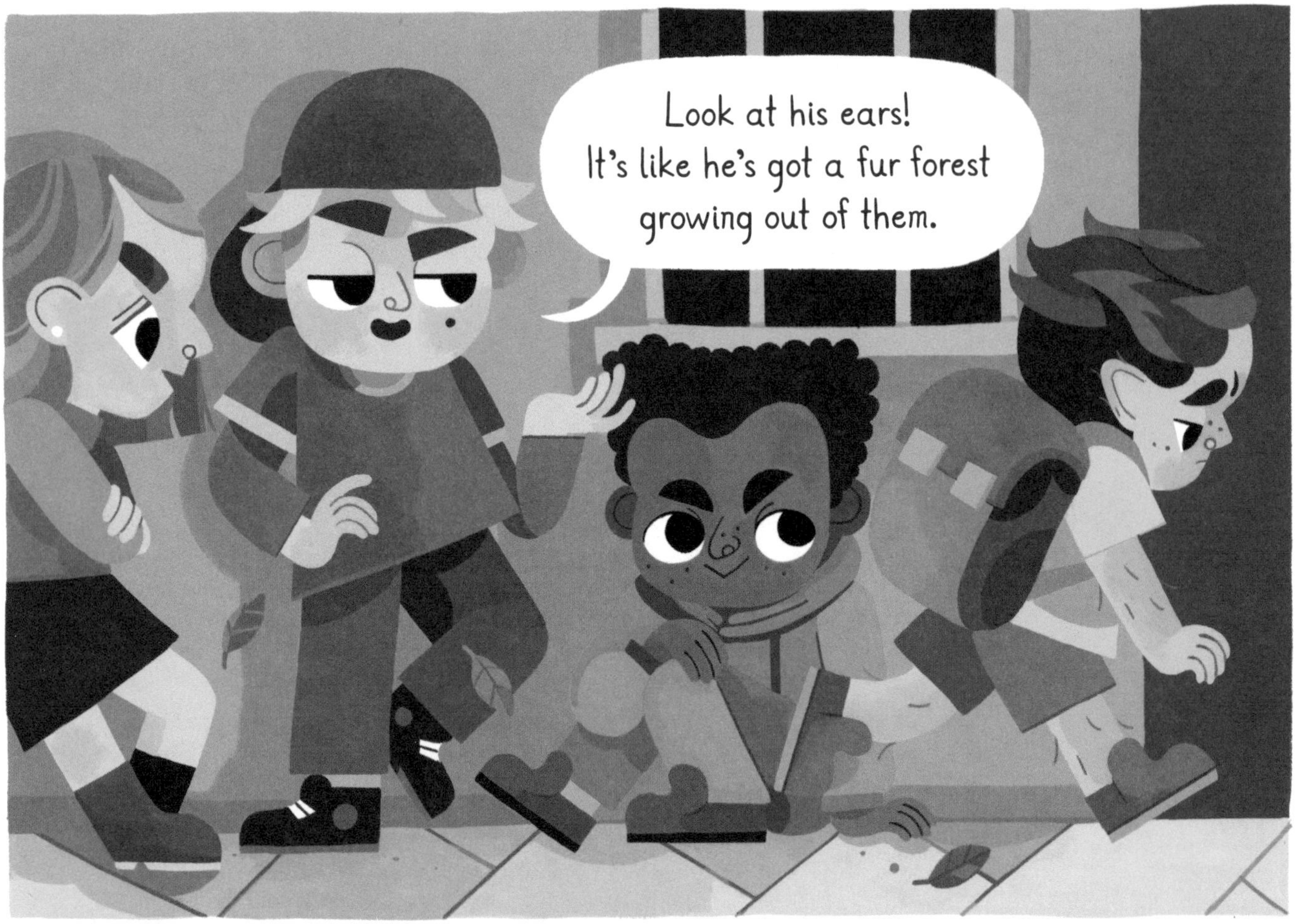
Look at his ears! It's like he's got a fur forest growing out of them.

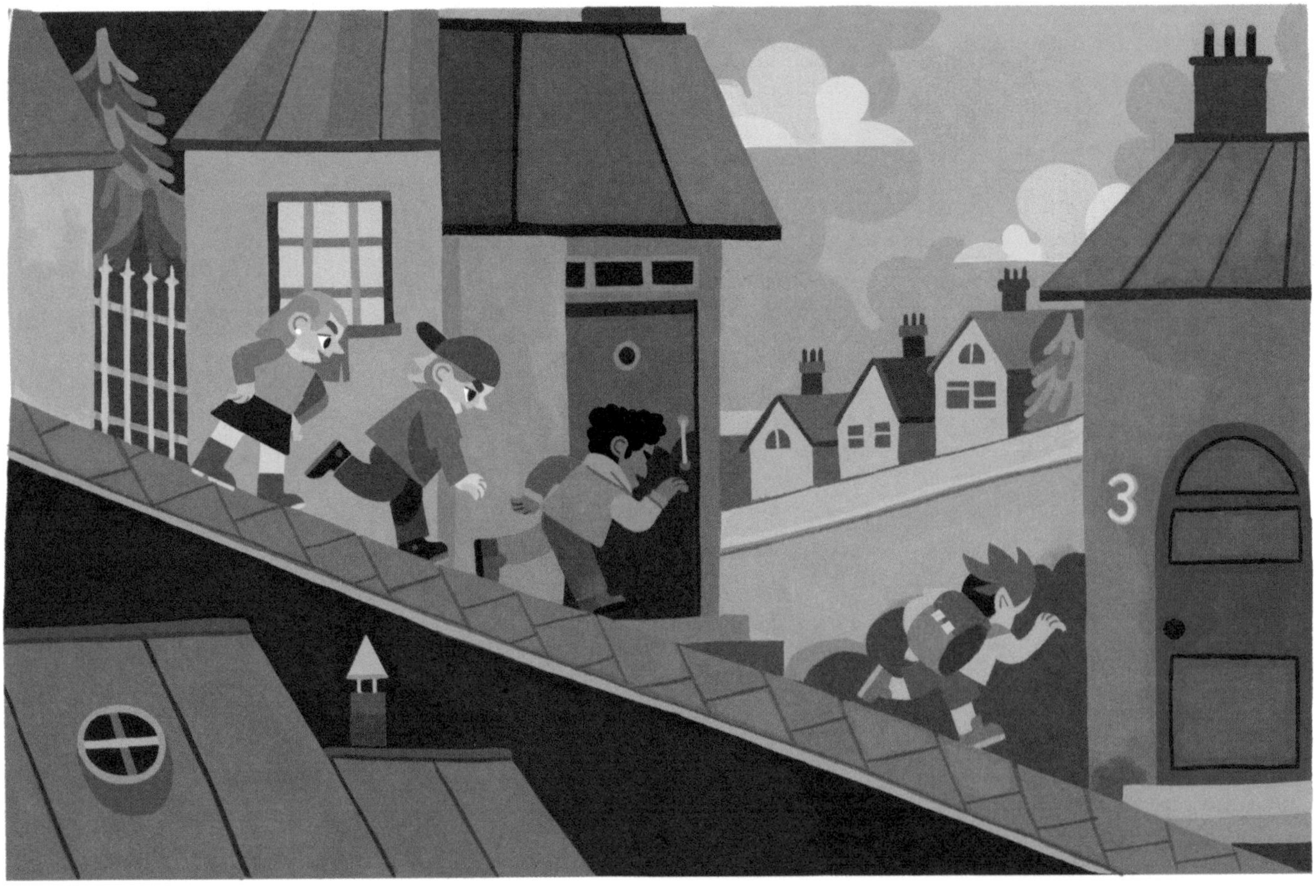
3

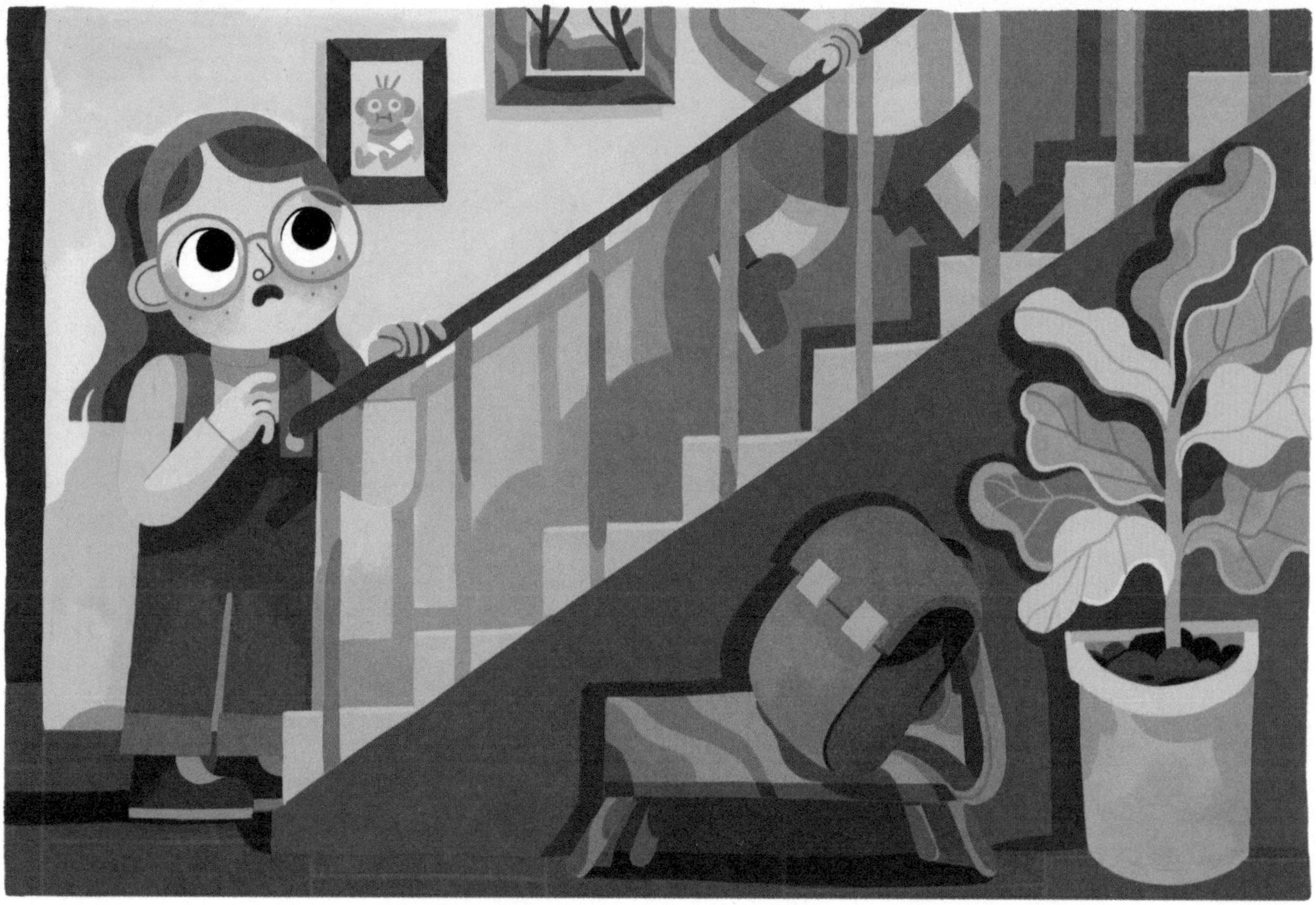

When he got home, he barricaded the door to his bedroom and buried his head under his blanket. Lowell just wanted to disappear. But Lys wouldn't let him.

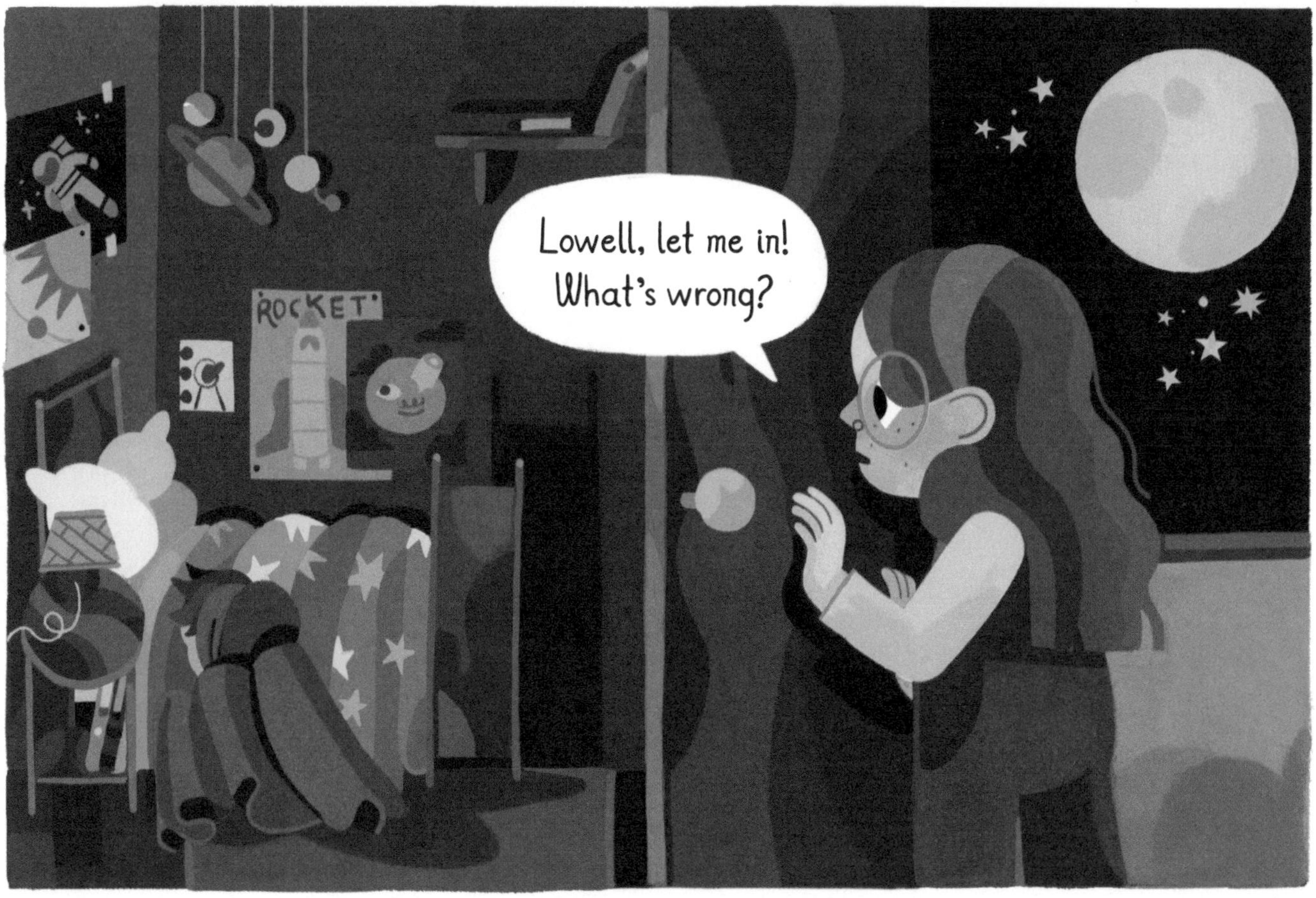
ROCKET
Lowell, let me in! What's wrong?

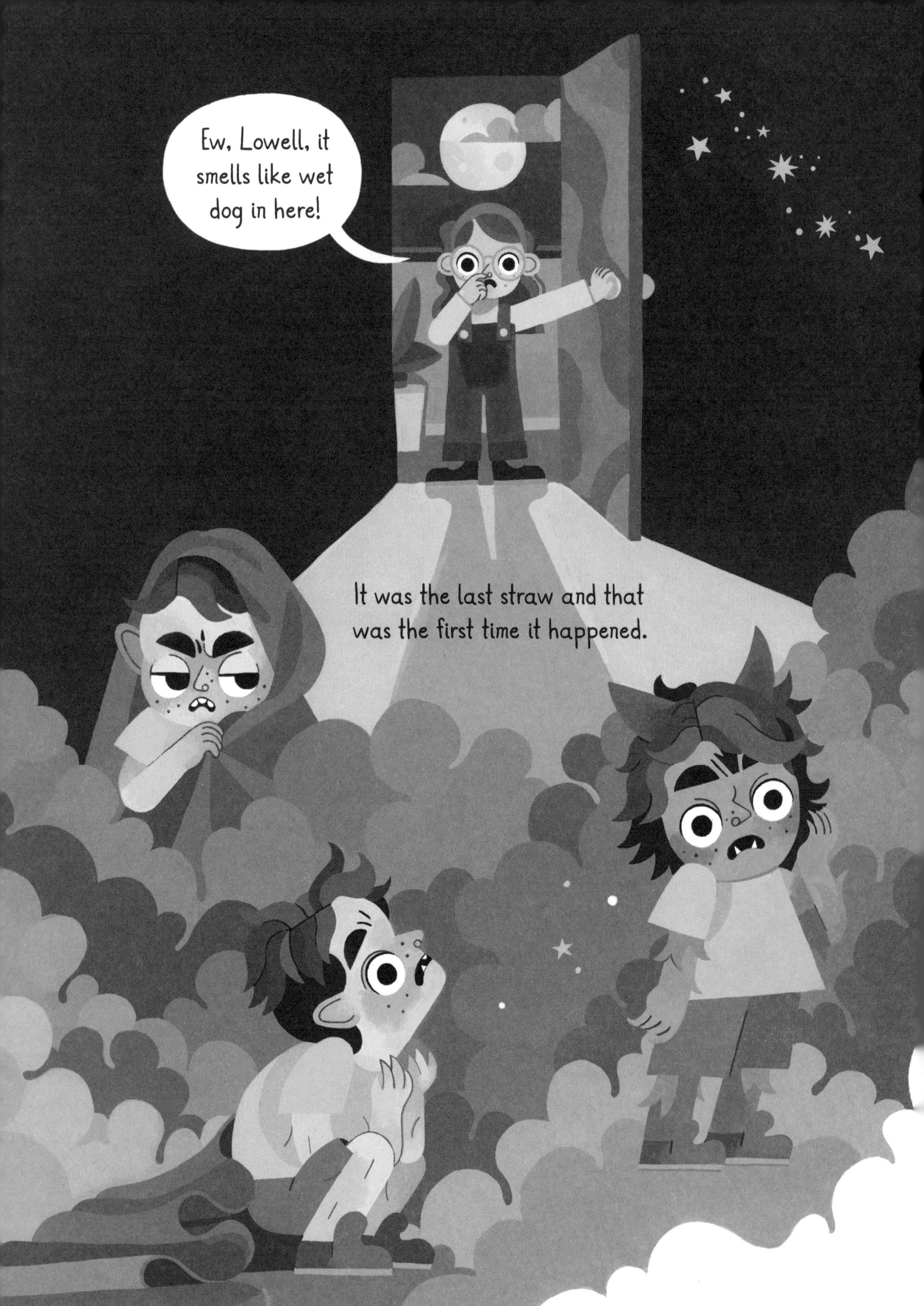
Ew, Lowell, it smells like wet dog in here!
It was the last straw and that was the first time it happened.

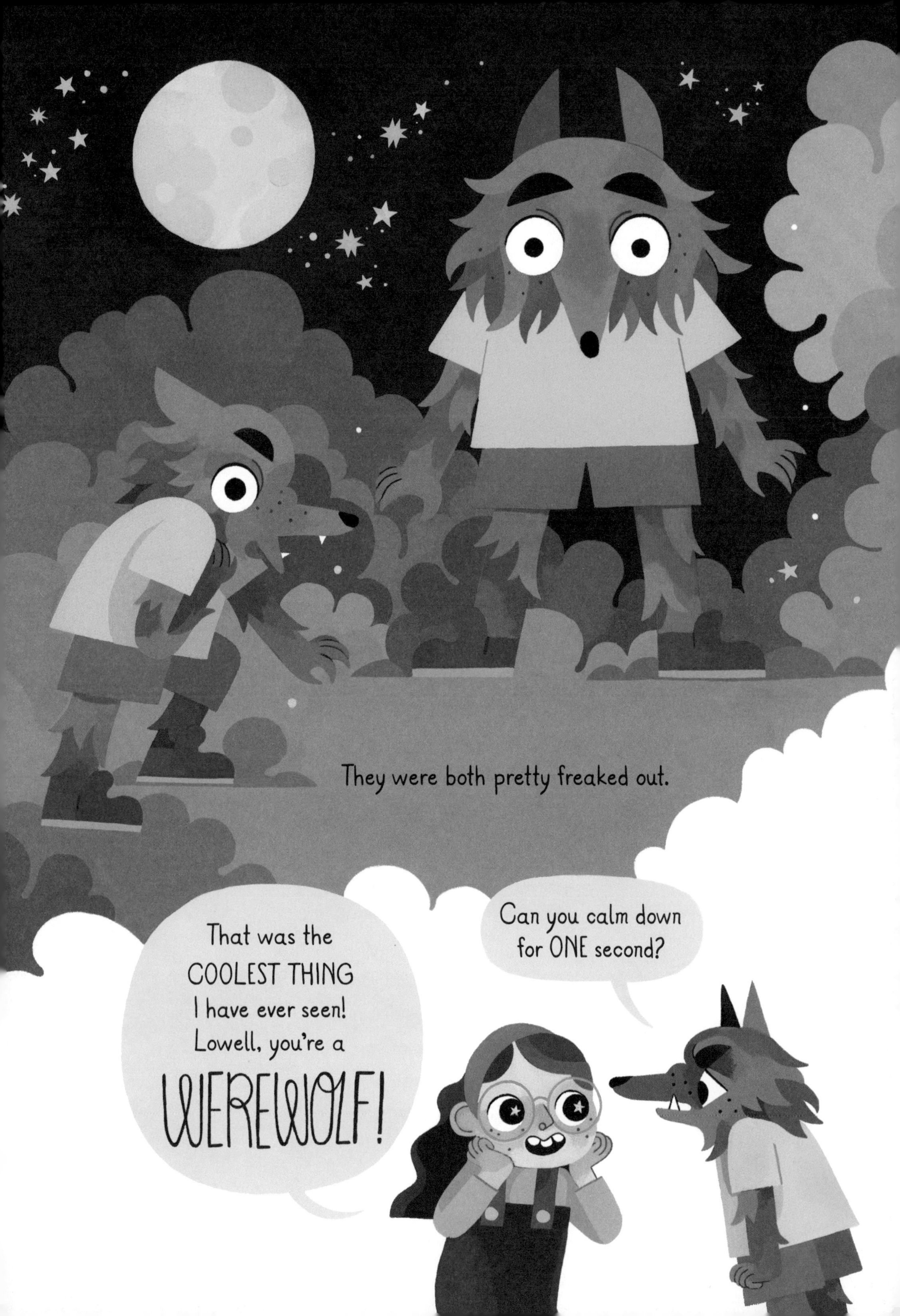
They were both pretty freaked out.
That was the COOLEST THING I have ever seen! Lowell, you're a WEREWOLF!
Can you calm down for ONE second?

A werewolf!? Maybe this was clearly just one of those weird growing up things. Maybe ALL boys went through these changes and nobody talked about it because it was so embarrassing.

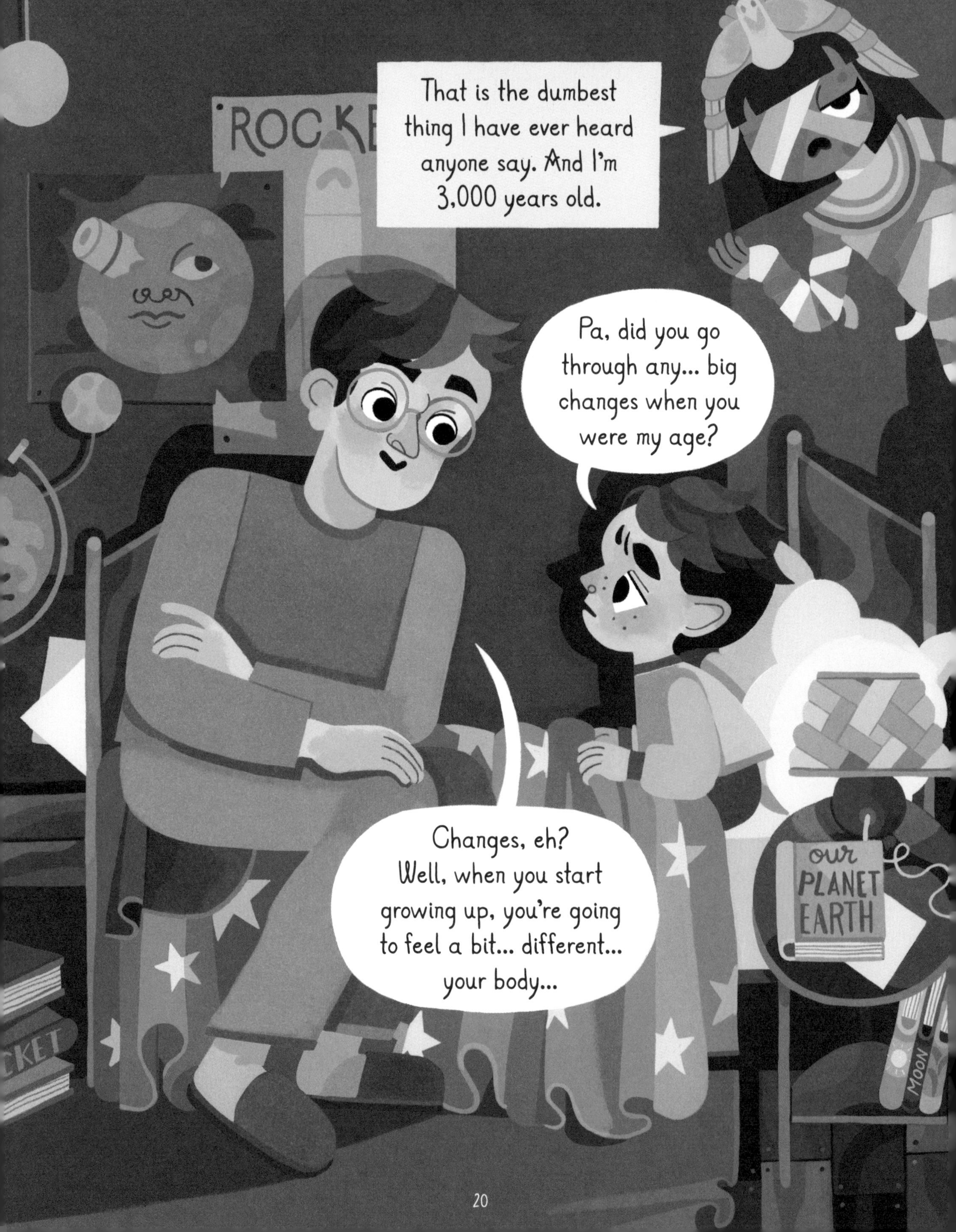
That is the dumbest thing I have ever heard anyone say. And I'm 3,000 years old.
ROCKE
Pa, did you go through any... big changes when you were my age?
Changes, eh? Well, when you start growing up, you're going to feel a bit... different... your body...
our PLANET EARTH
MOON

The conversation got very odd, very quickly. I'll spare you the details, but no, Pa hadn't transformed into a monster. He had gone through a lot of other weird stuff.

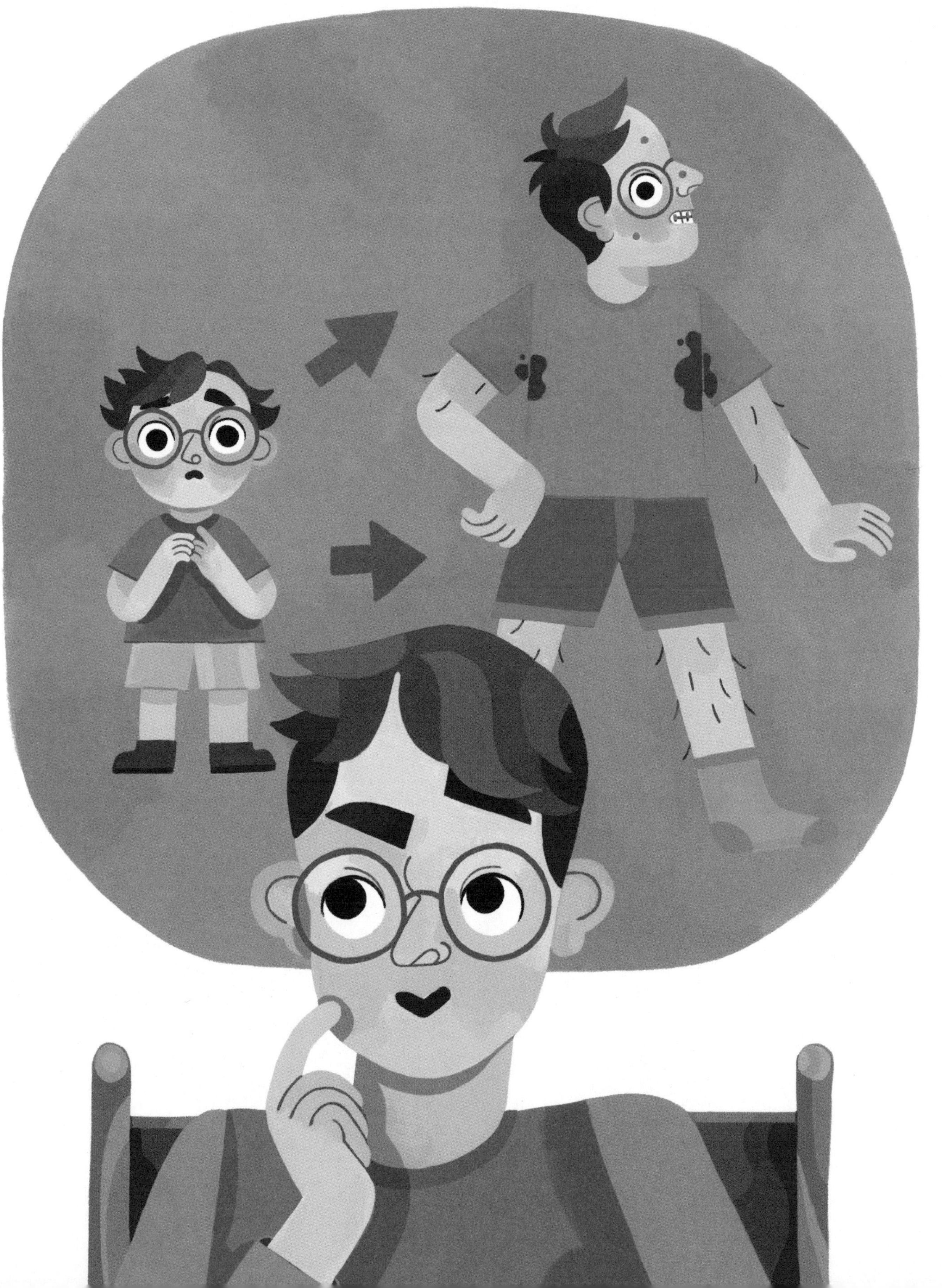

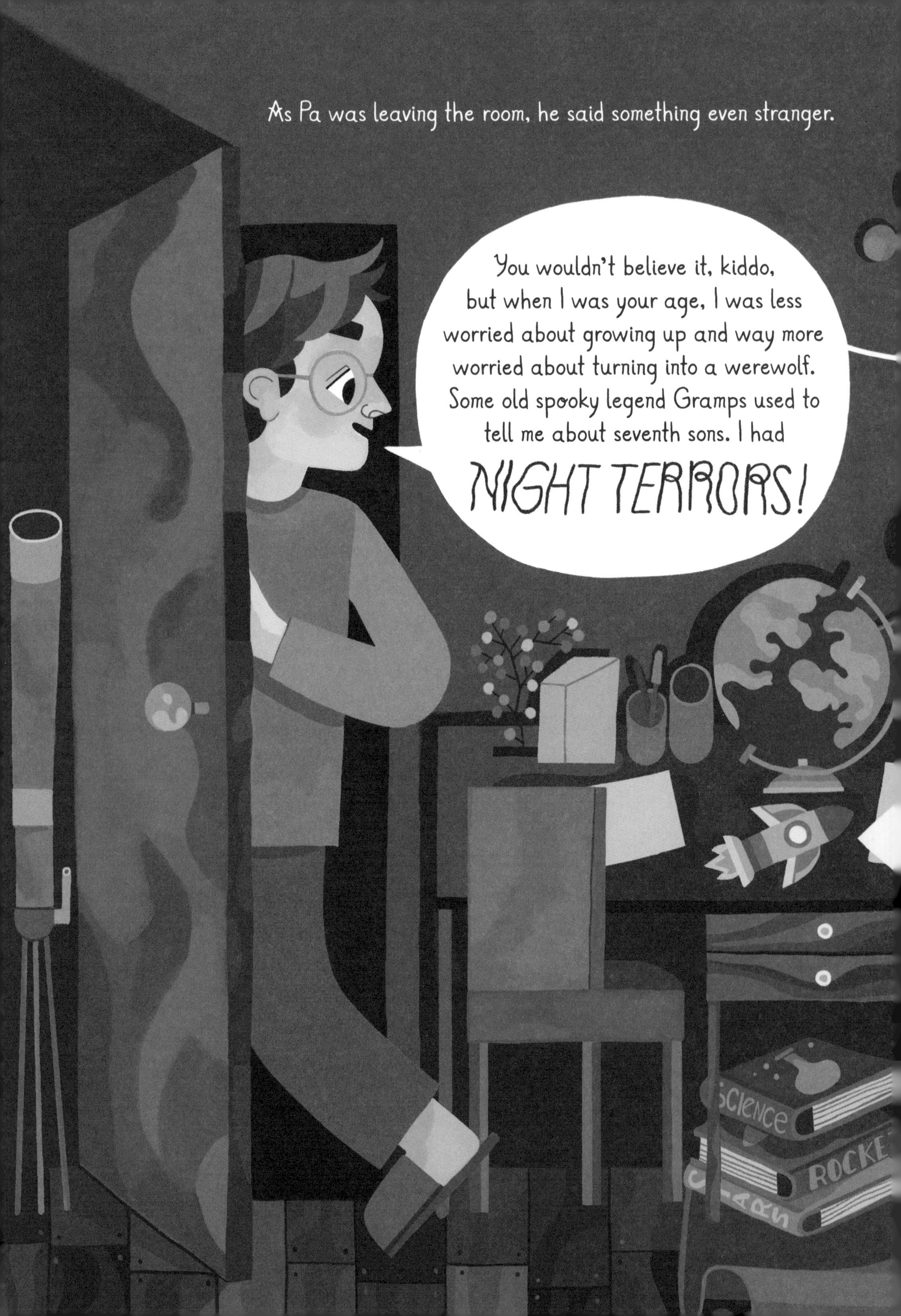
As Pa was leaving the room, he said something even stranger.
You wouldn't believe it, kiddo, but when I was your age, I was less worried about growing up and way more worried about turning into a werewolf. Some old spooky legend Gramps used to tell me about seventh sons. I had NIGHT TERRORS!
SCIENCE

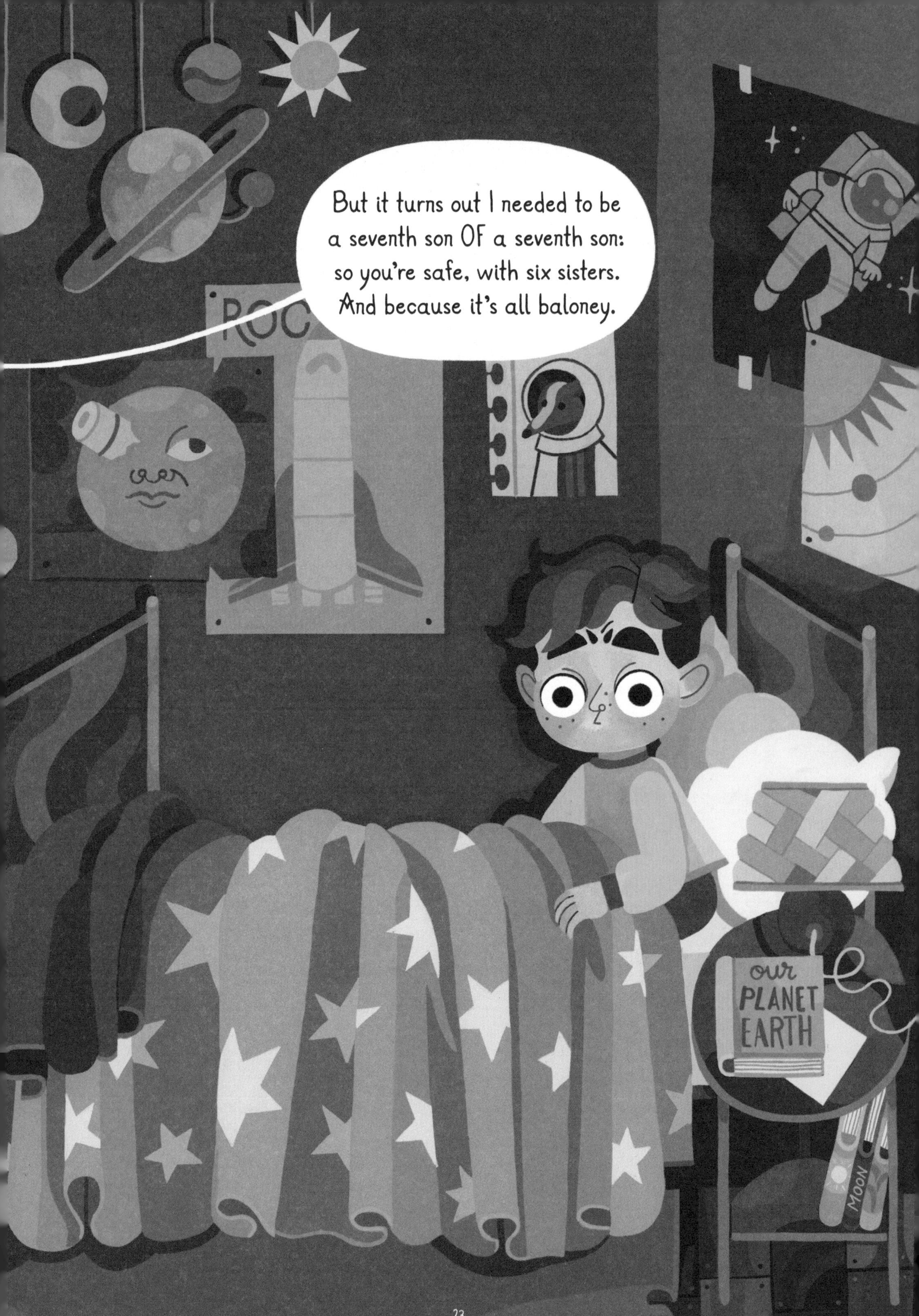
But it turns out I needed to be a seventh son OF a seventh son: so you're safe, with six sisters. And because it's all baloney.
ROC
our PLANET EARTH
MOON

The next morning, Lowell told Lys what Pa had said. She was BEYOND excited.

They met up in the library and she grabbed as many spooky books off the shelves as she could.

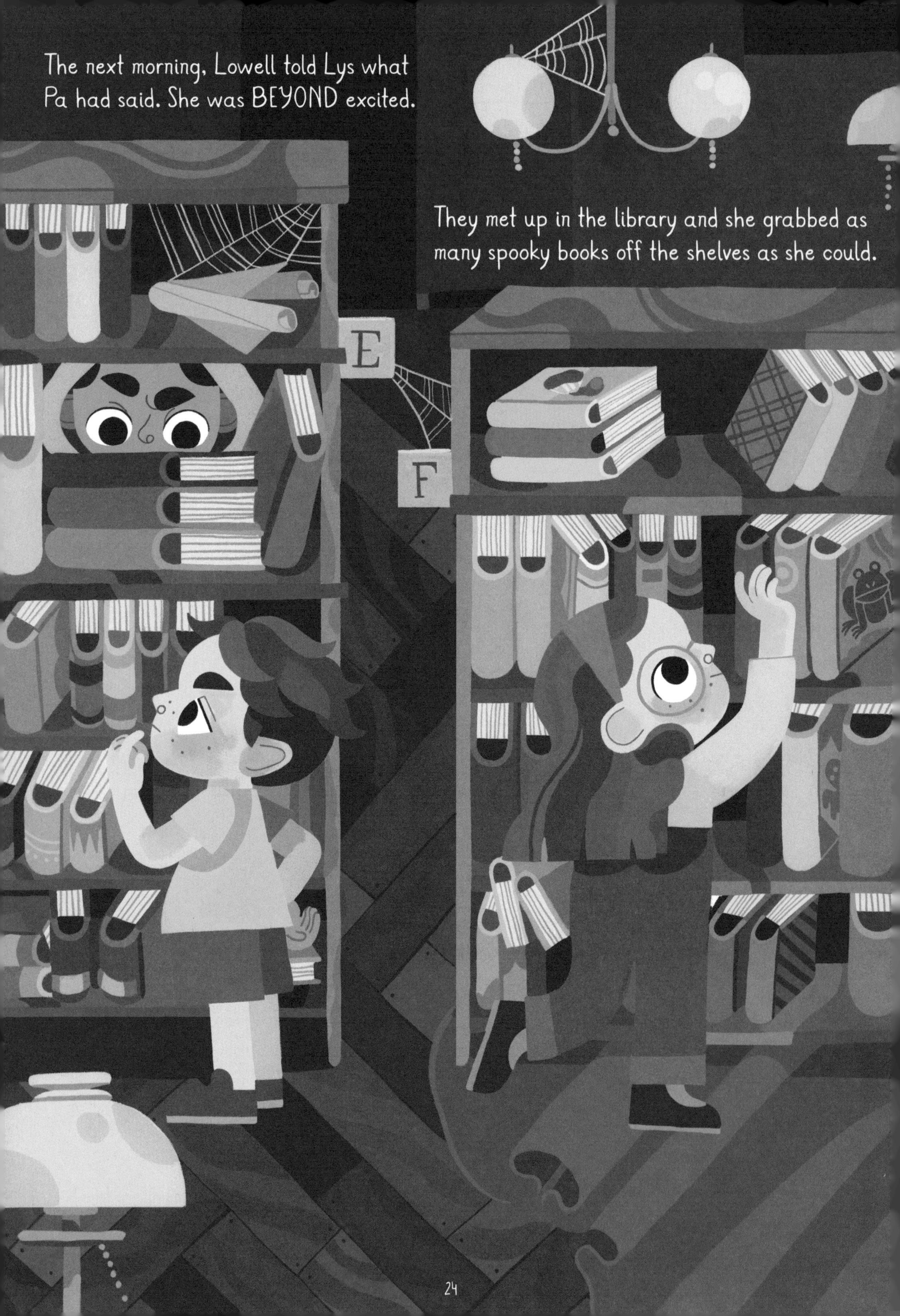
E
F

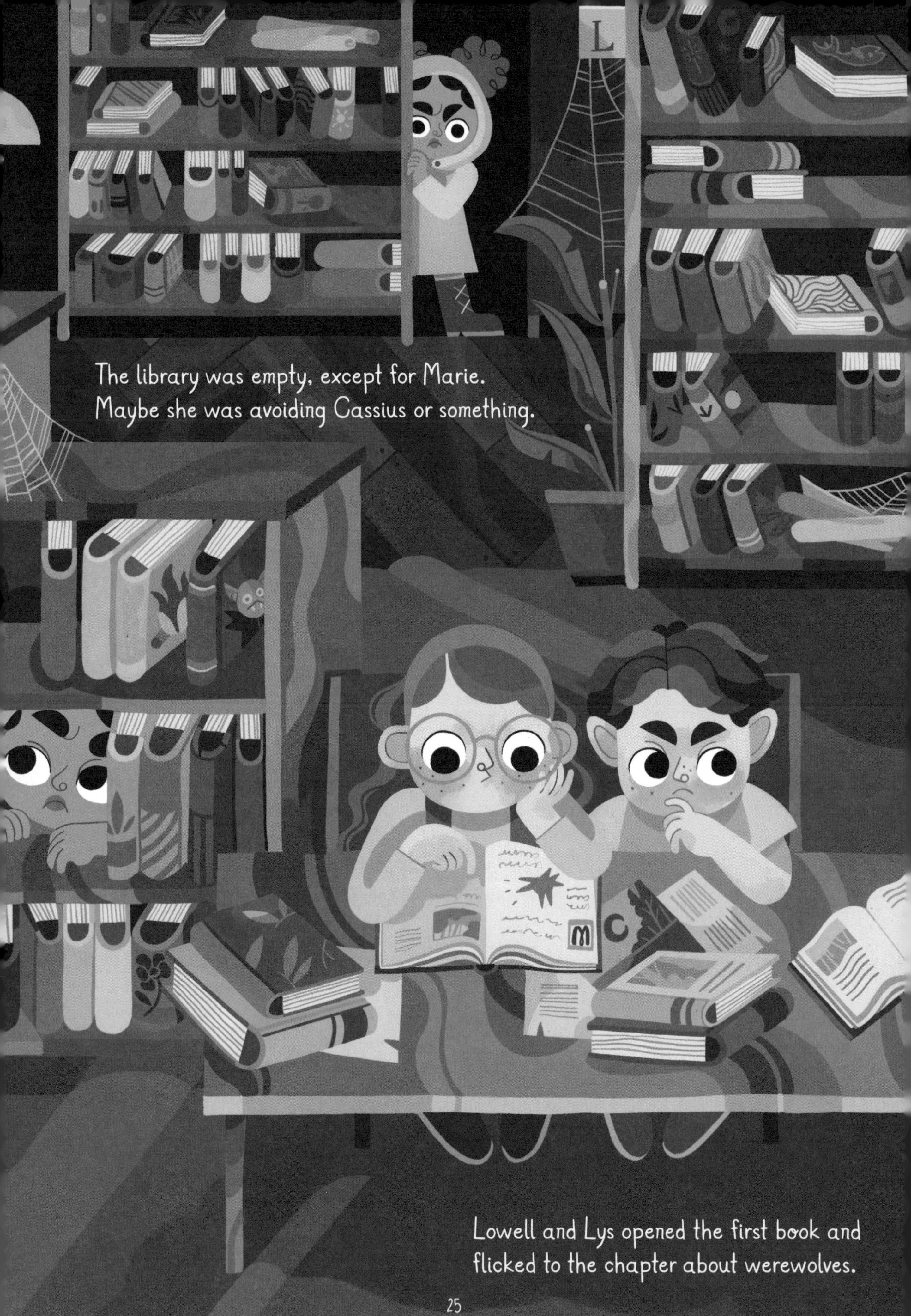

The library was empty, except for Marie.
Maybe she was avoiding Cassius or something.

Lowell and Lys opened the first book and
flicked to the chapter about werewolves.

TALE OF LYCAON

In ancient Arcadia, there was a cruel king named Lycaon. He built a towering temple in honour of Zeus where he made gory human sacrifices in his name. High atop his home on Mount Olympus, Zeus heard rumours of what was going on and decided to pay Lycaon a visit. Only, he went in disguise.

Lycaon cooked up a feast for his mysterious guest, with sweet honey, warm bread and a centrepiece of human flesh.

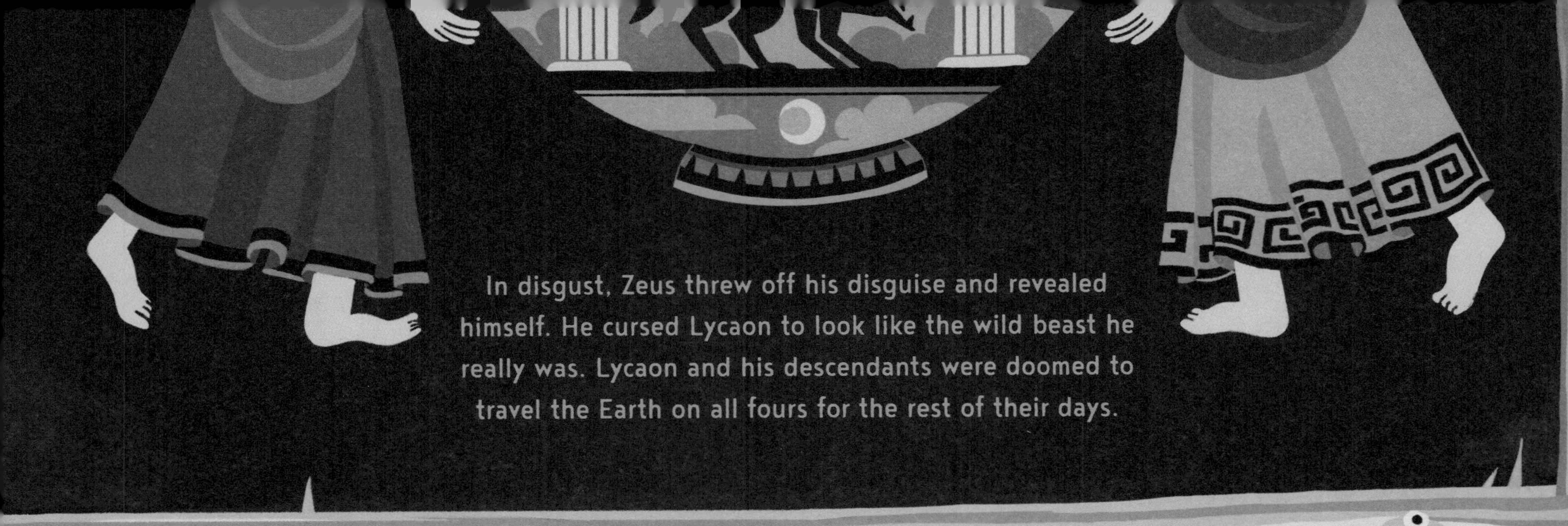

In disgust, Zeus threw off his disguise and revealed himself. He cursed Lycaon to look like the wild beast he really was. Lycaon and his descendants were doomed to travel the Earth on all fours for the rest of their days.

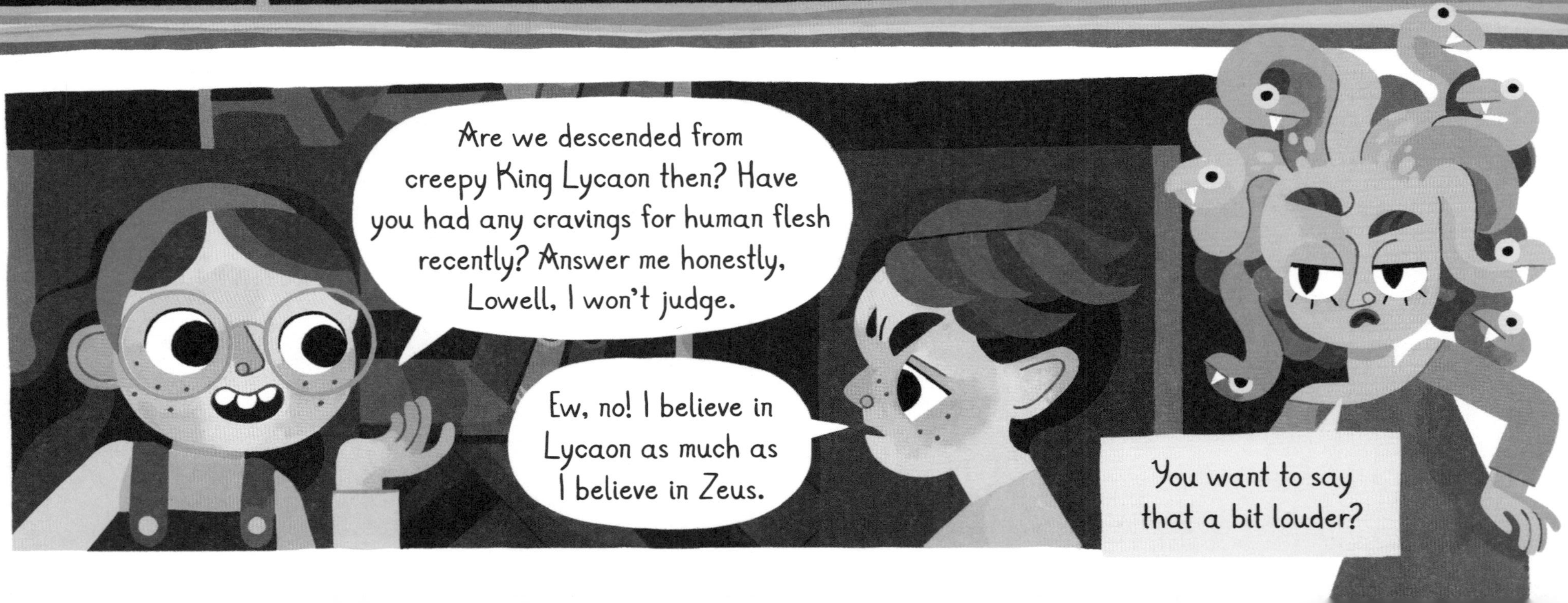
Are we descended from creepy King Lycaon then? Have you had any cravings for human flesh recently? Answer me honestly, Lowell, I won't judge.
Ew, no! I believe in Lycaon as much as I believe in Zeus.
You want to say that a bit louder?

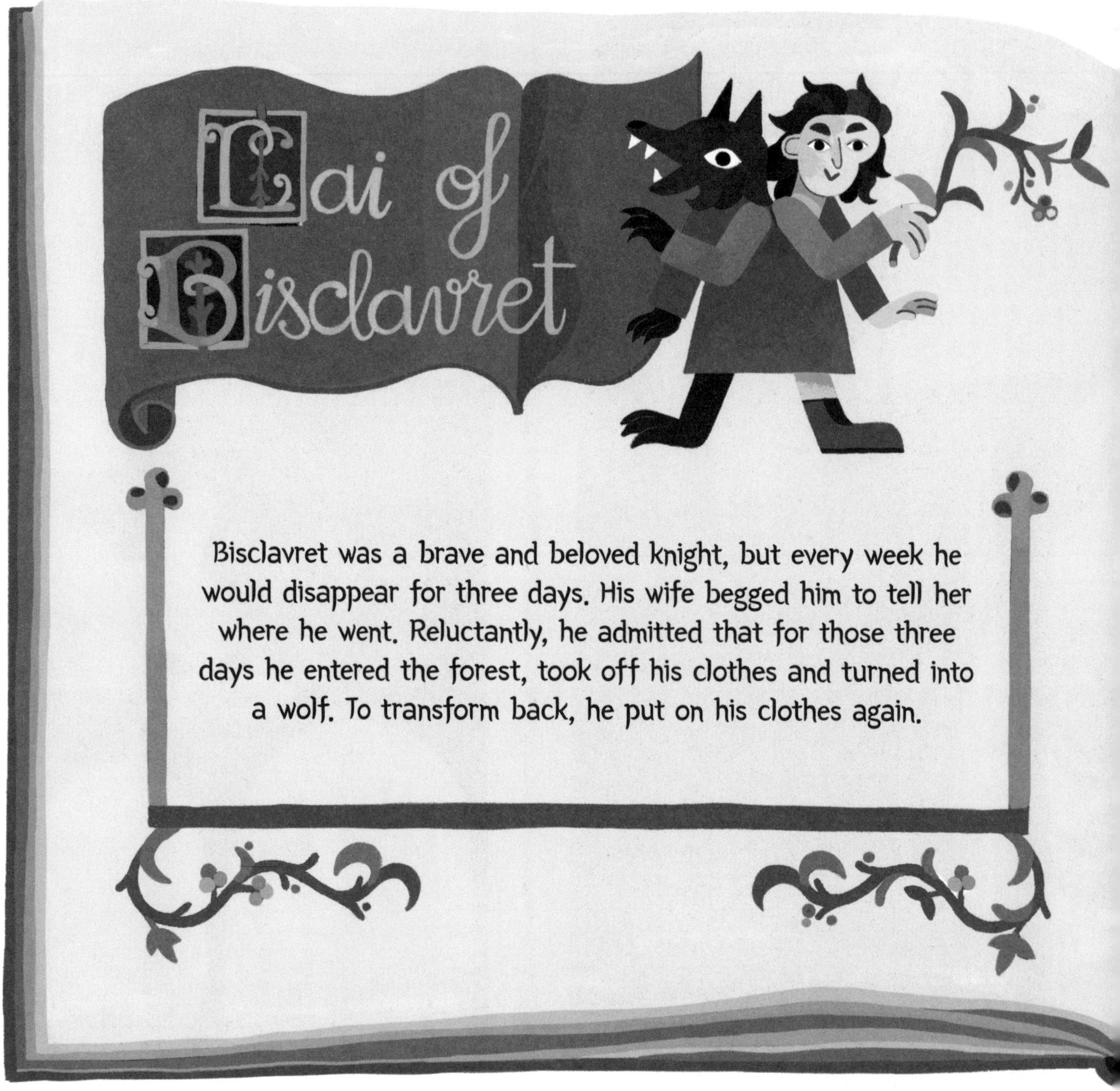
Lai of Bisclavret
Bisclavret was a brave and beloved knight, but every week he would disappear for three days. His wife begged him to tell her where he went. Reluctantly, he admitted that for those three days he entered the forest, took off his clothes and turned into a wolf. To transform back, he put on his clothes again.

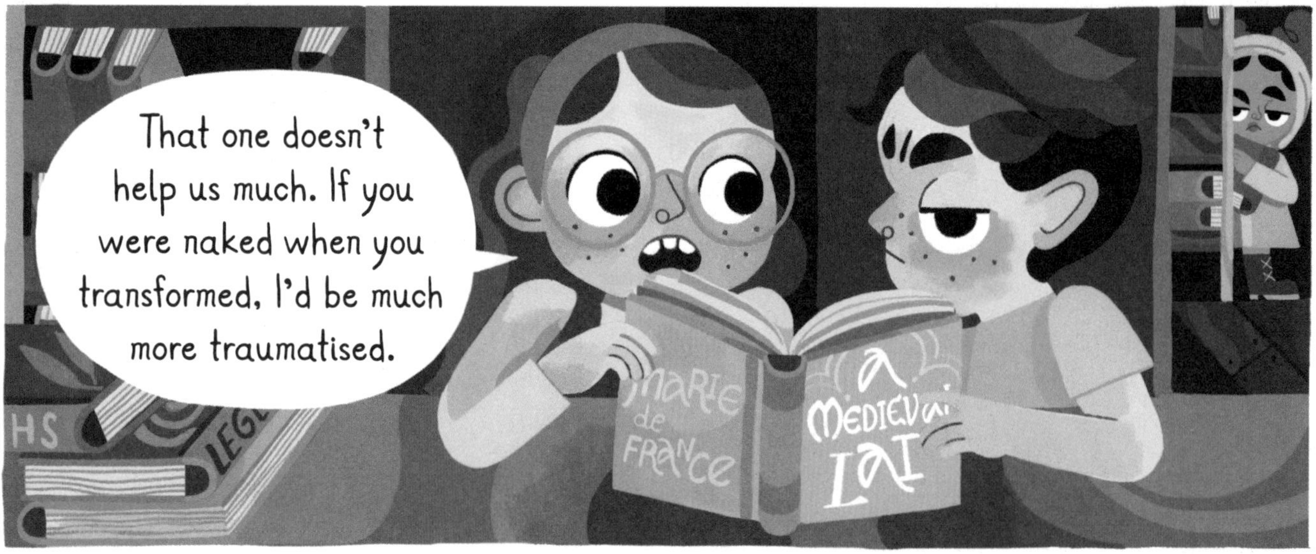
That one doesn't help us much. If you were naked when you transformed, I'd be much more traumatised.
Marie de France

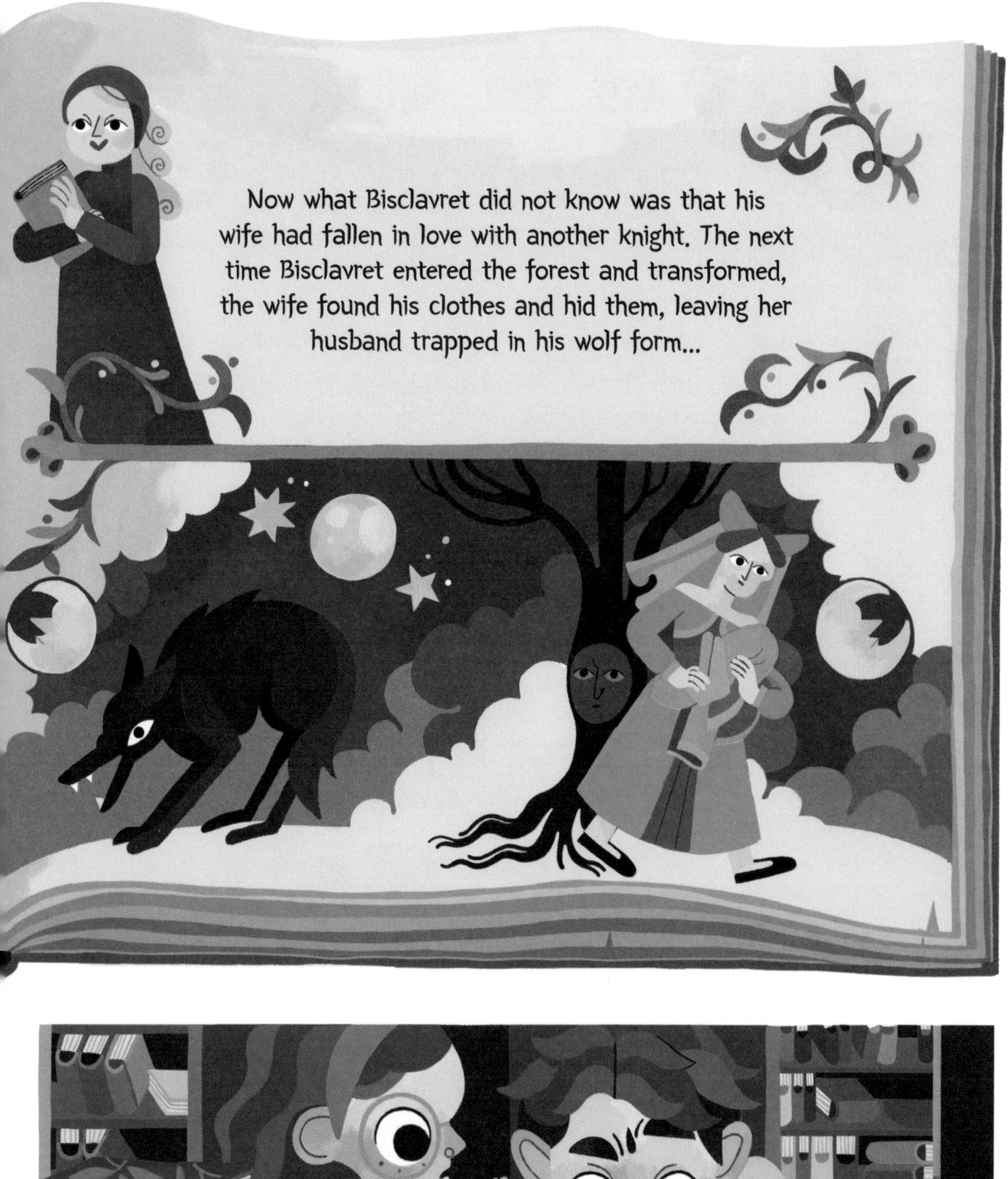
Now what Bisclavret did not know was that his wife had fallen in love with another knight. The next time Bisclavret entered the forest and transformed, the wife found his clothes and hid them, leaving her husband trapped in his wolf form...

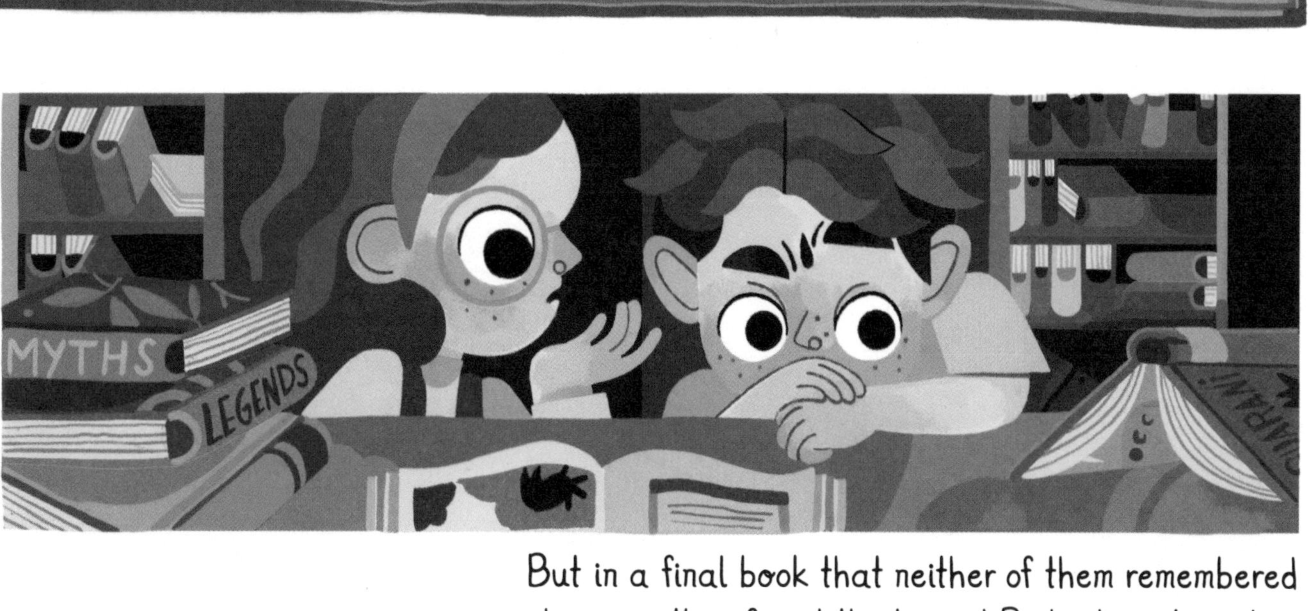
MYTHS
LEGENDS

But in a final book that neither of them remembered choosing, they found the legend Pa had mentioned.

LoBisón

If he is a seventh son of a seventh son, and if the wolfblood runs strong through his lineage, then on the cusp of manhood, hair shall join betwixt his brows, fur sprout from his ears, claws grow from his fingertips and 'neath the full moon, shall he be a beast!

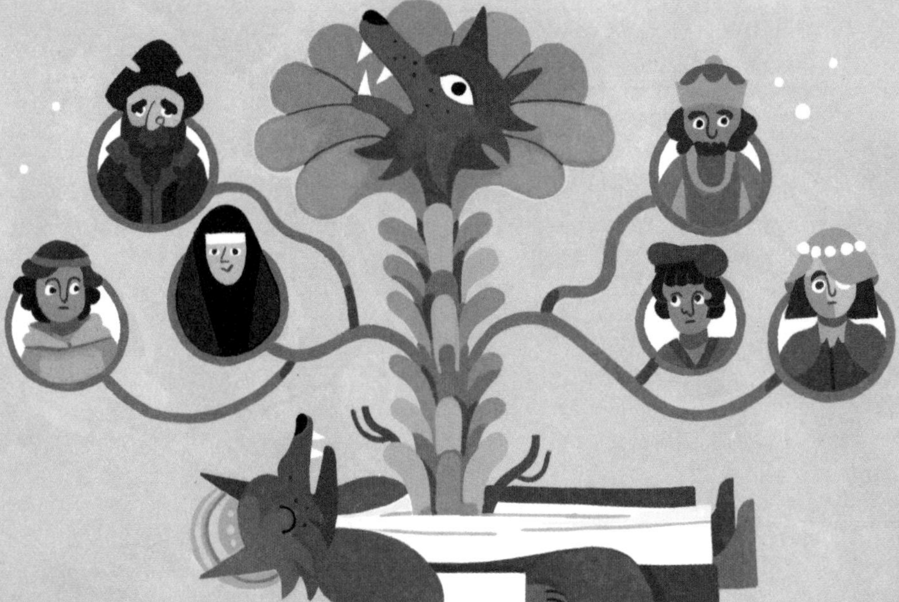

note: If the wolfblood runs with great strength in a family, then the curse can afflict any seventh child of a seventh son, be they male or female, have they brothers or sisters.

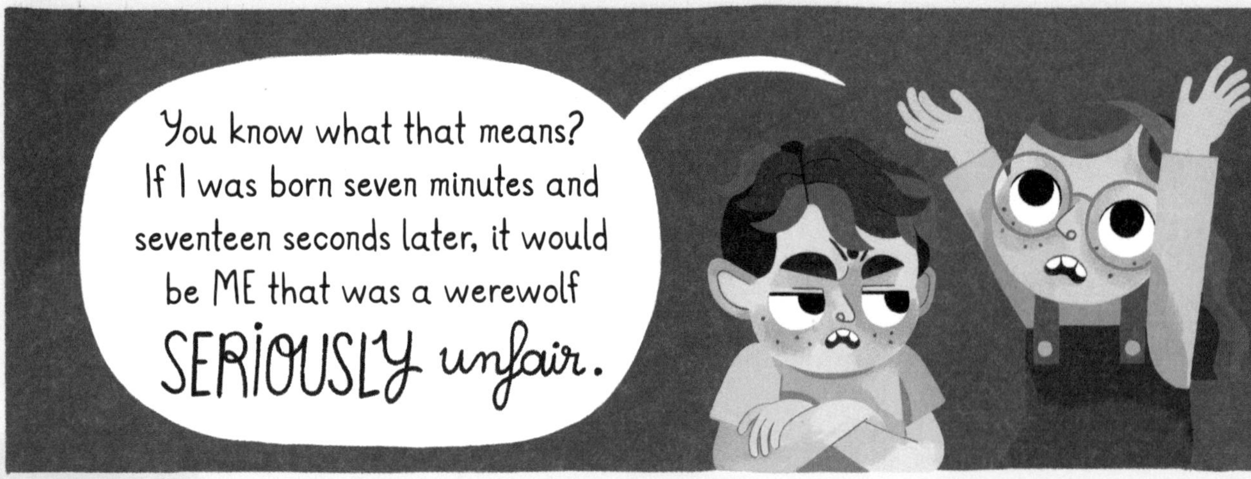
You know what that means? If I was born seven minutes and seventeen seconds later, it would be ME that was a werewolf SERIOUSLY unfair.

To cure thyself of the werewolf curse, blend a batch of
Potion Personalis, which will turn thee back to thy true self.
This potion can only be prepared by a practising witch
and must be brewed on the full moon. If all the hags in thy
village have been imprisoned, banished or burned at
the stake, thy could try one of these rituals instead...

To begin with, Lys was less than keen to try any of the so-called cures. She thought being a werewolf was a gift, not a curse. She wasn't the one with giant furry eyebrows though.

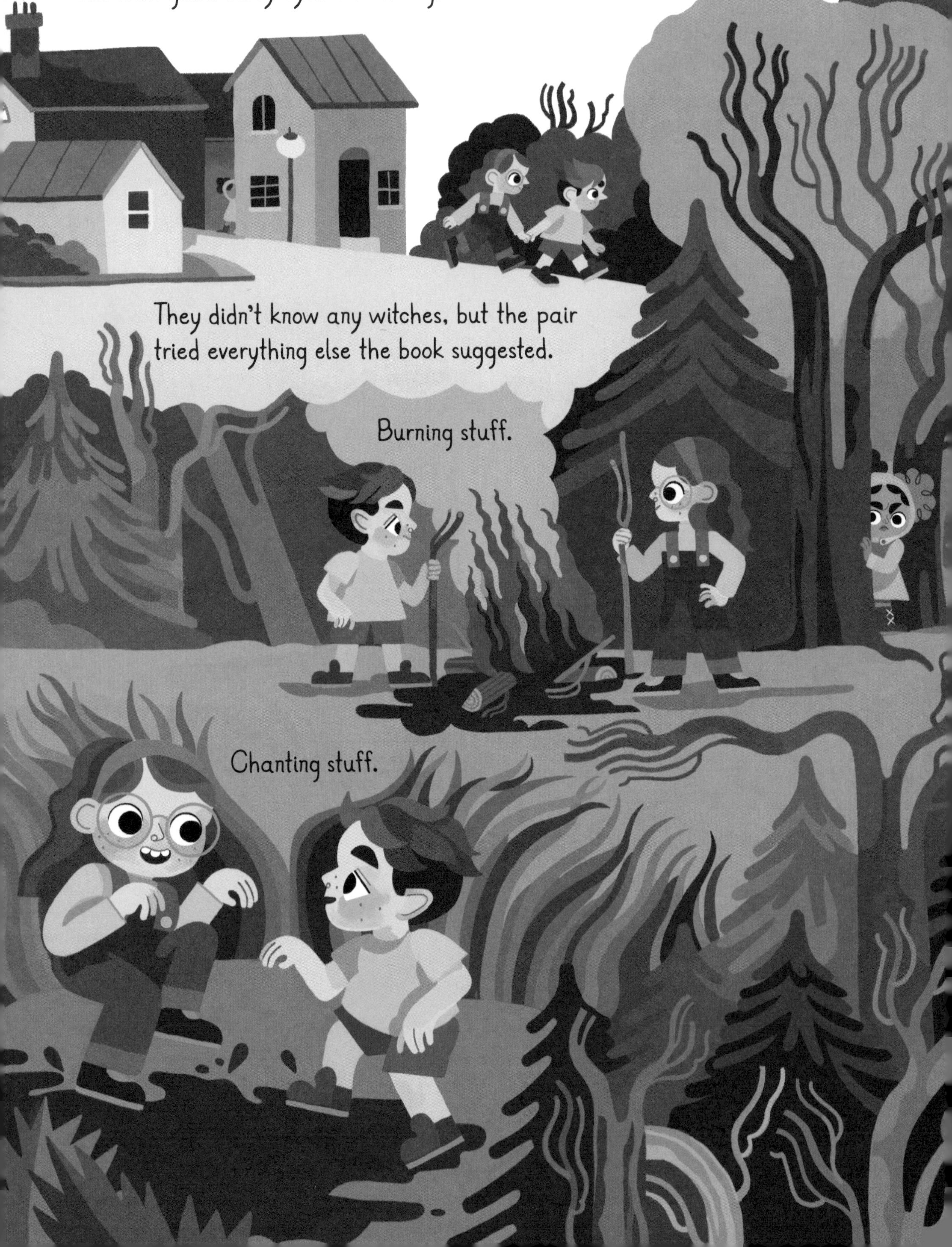

They didn't know any witches, but the pair tried everything else the book suggested.

Burning stuff.

Chanting stuff.

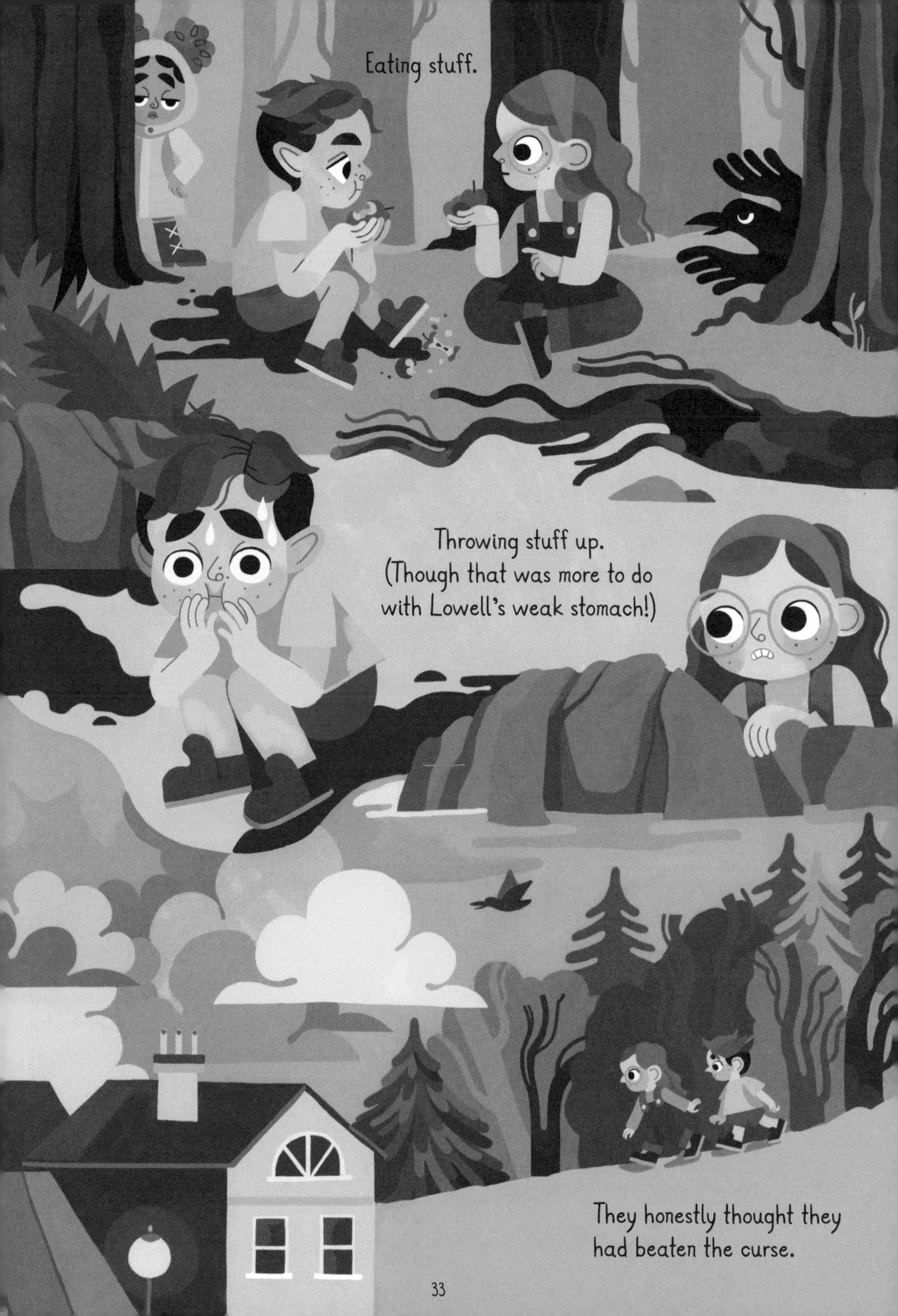

Eating stuff.

Throwing stuff up.
(Though that was more to do with Lowell's weak stomach!)

They honestly thought they had beaten the curse.

The days slipped by until it had been a full month since Lowell's first monster makeover. Then the full moon rose...

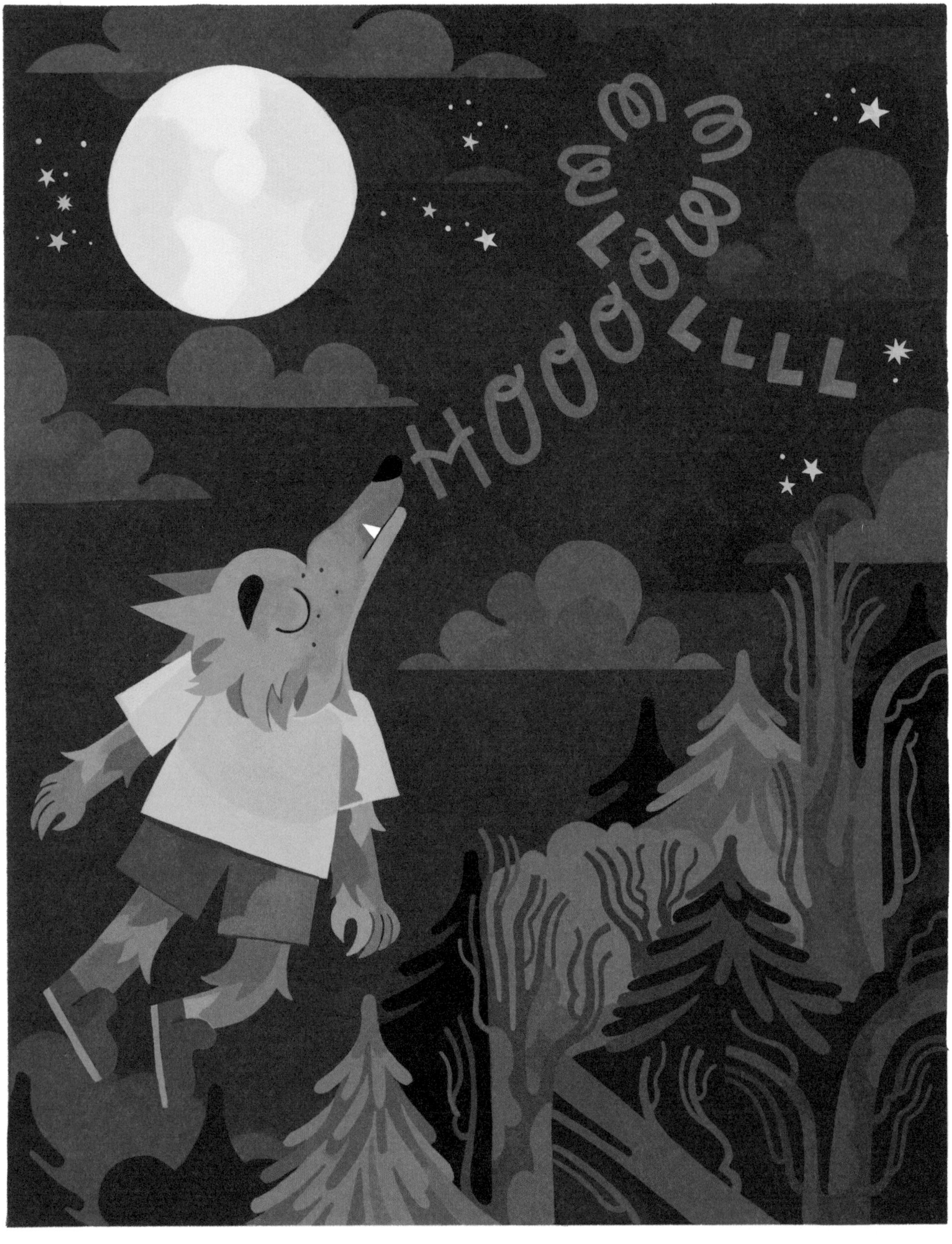
HOOOOOOWWWWWLLLLL

Long story short, the "cures" hadn't worked.

The night sky felt close enough to touch. For a moment there, everything felt sparkly and special.

Then Lowell nearly ran into Cassius and his cronies – they were trying to shove Marie in a bin but somehow she disappeared.

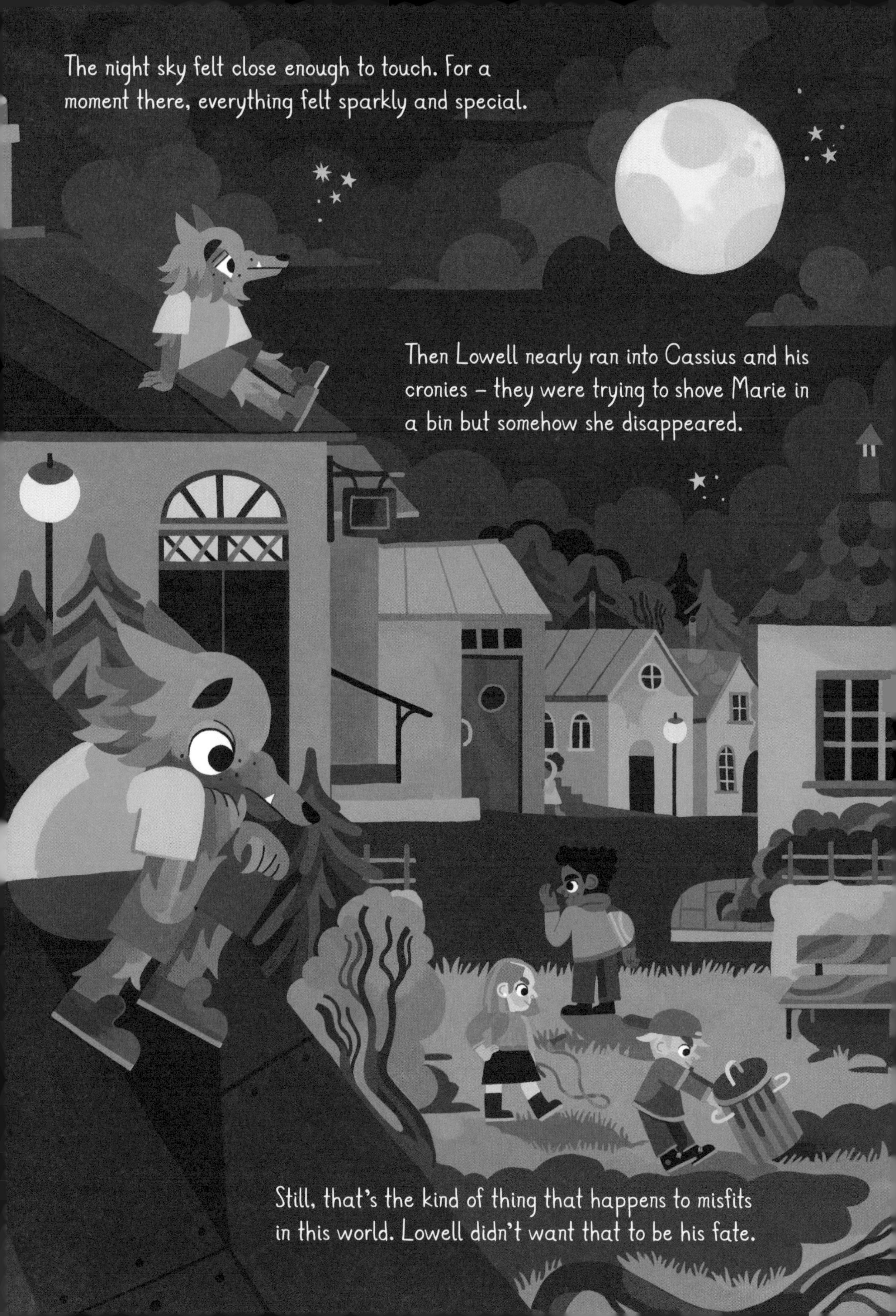

Still, that's the kind of thing that happens to misfits in this world. Lowell didn't want that to be his fate.

Lowell and Lys decided they had to do something.
They caught a night bus to the big library in town.

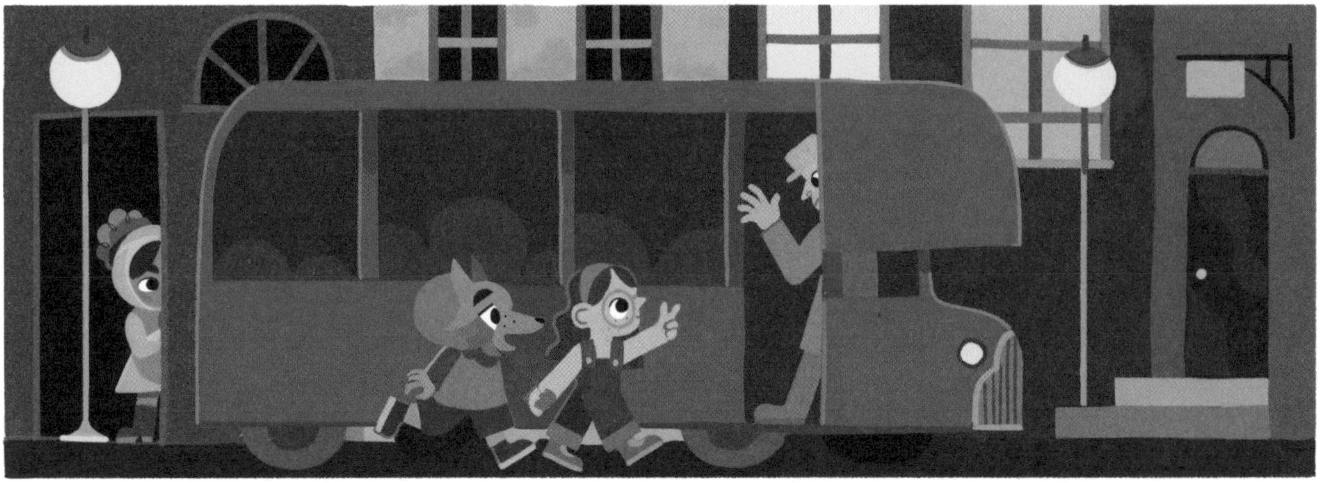

They hoped to find something that might help Lowell change back.
A compendium of werewolf cures, a directory of local witches.

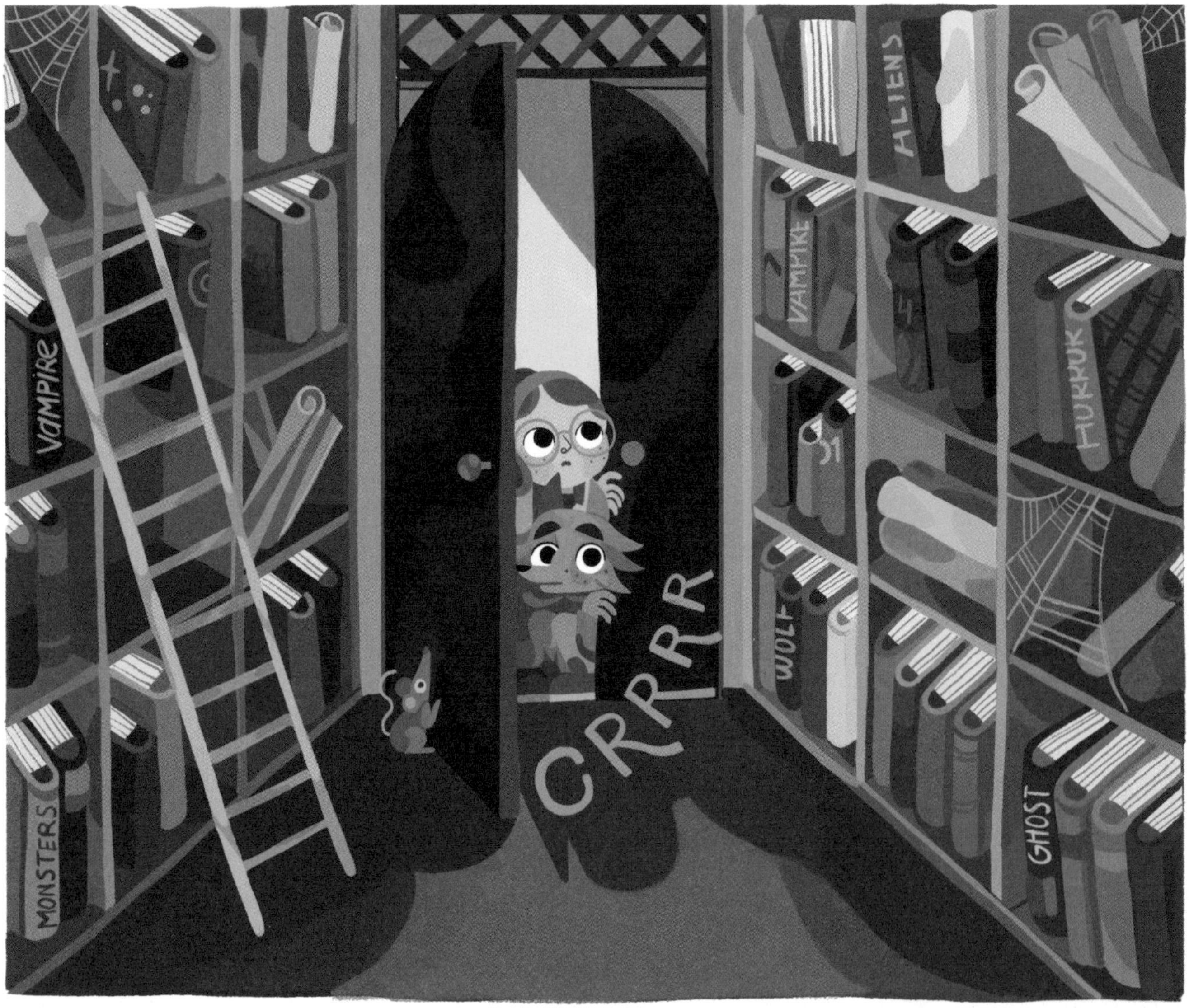
VAMPIRE
MONSTERS
ALIENS
VAMPIRE
HORROR
WOLF
GHOST
CRRRR

Something. ANYTHING.

It was locked up but Lowell was desperate, so they broke in.
In the Mythical Creatures section, they spotted this poster...

MONSTER support **GROUP**

Come one, come ghoul!
Meets monthly on the
night of the full moon
at witching hour.

He didn't want to go to any monster meeting
– Lowell wasn't really a monster. But Lys thought
there might be a witch there who could help them.

So Lowell finished telling his story.

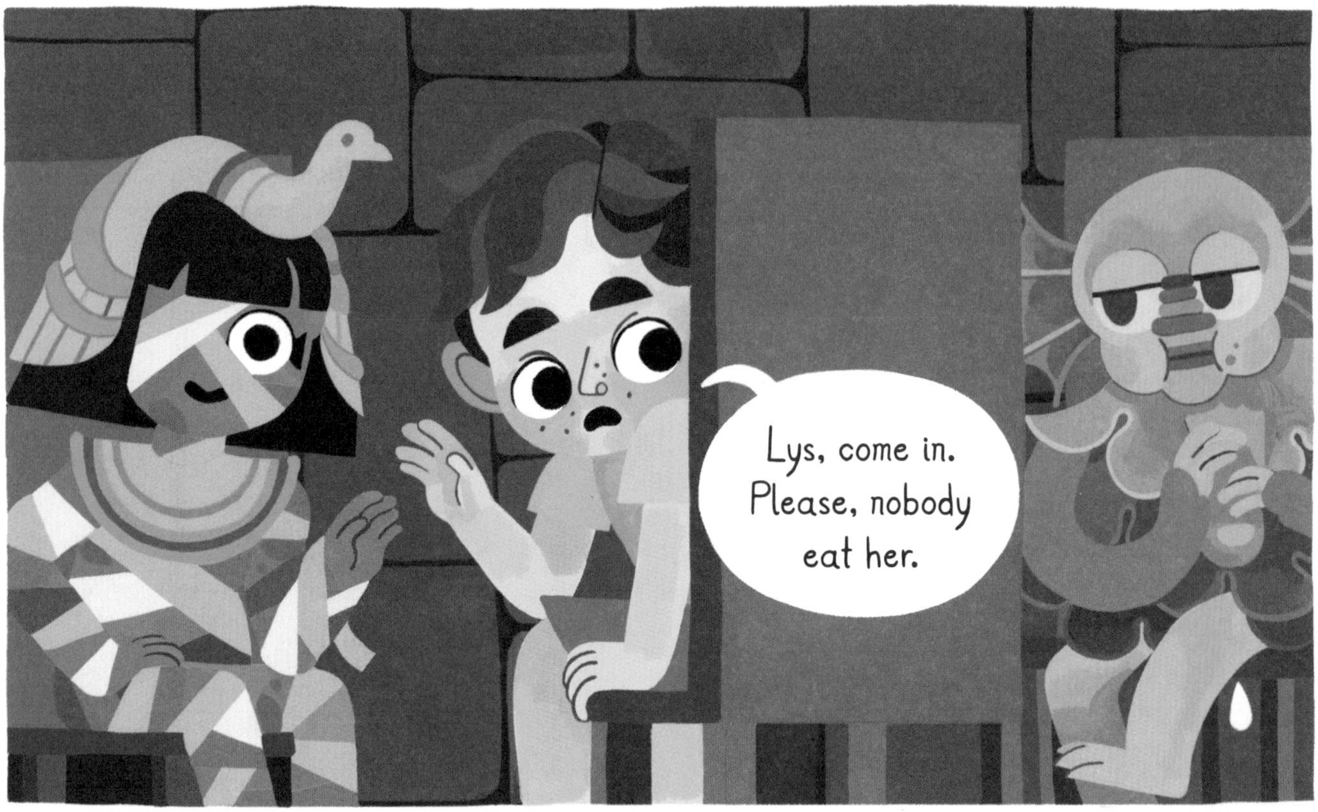
Lys, come in. Please, nobody eat her.

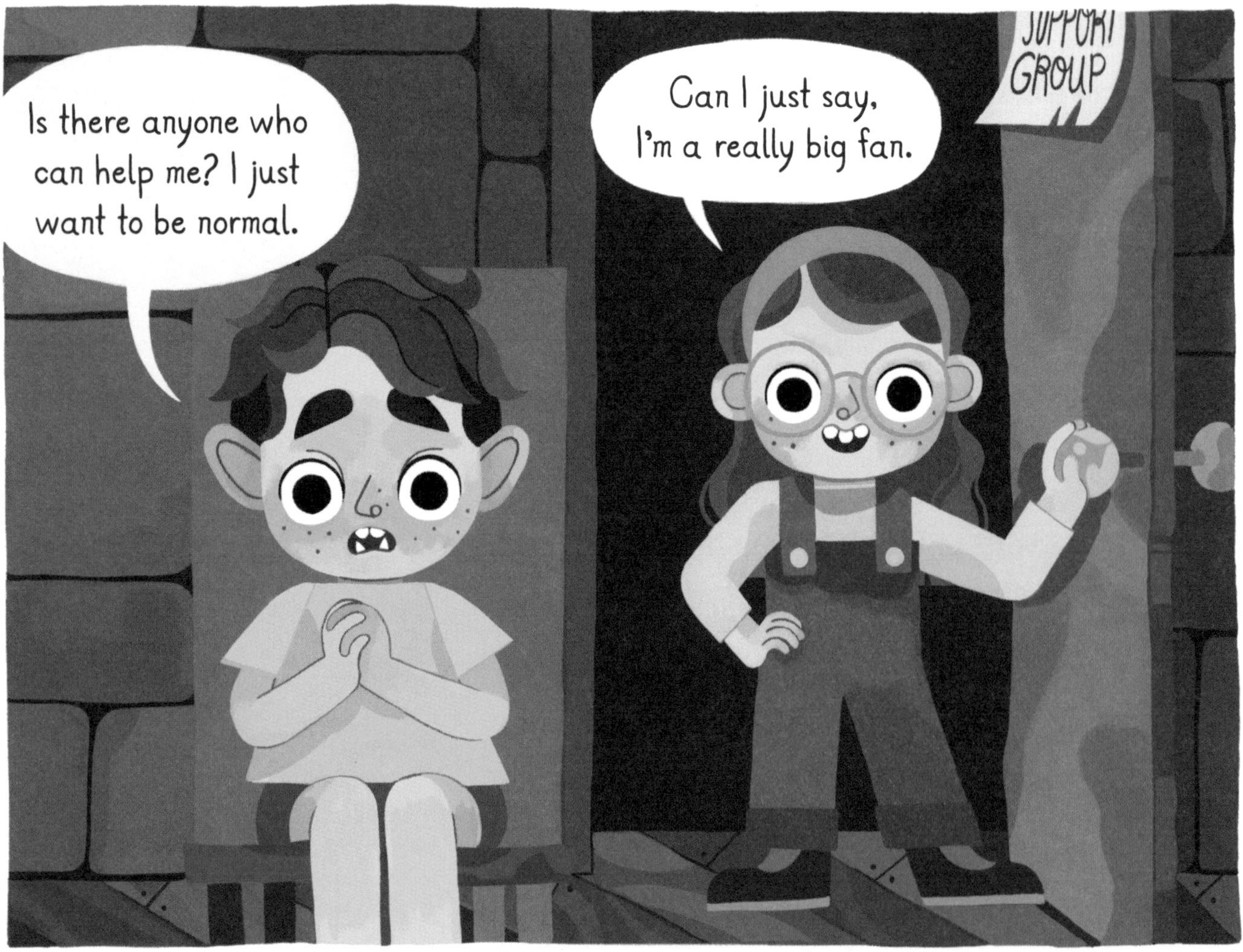
Is there anyone who can help me? I just want to be normal.
Can I just say, I'm a really big fan.
GROUP

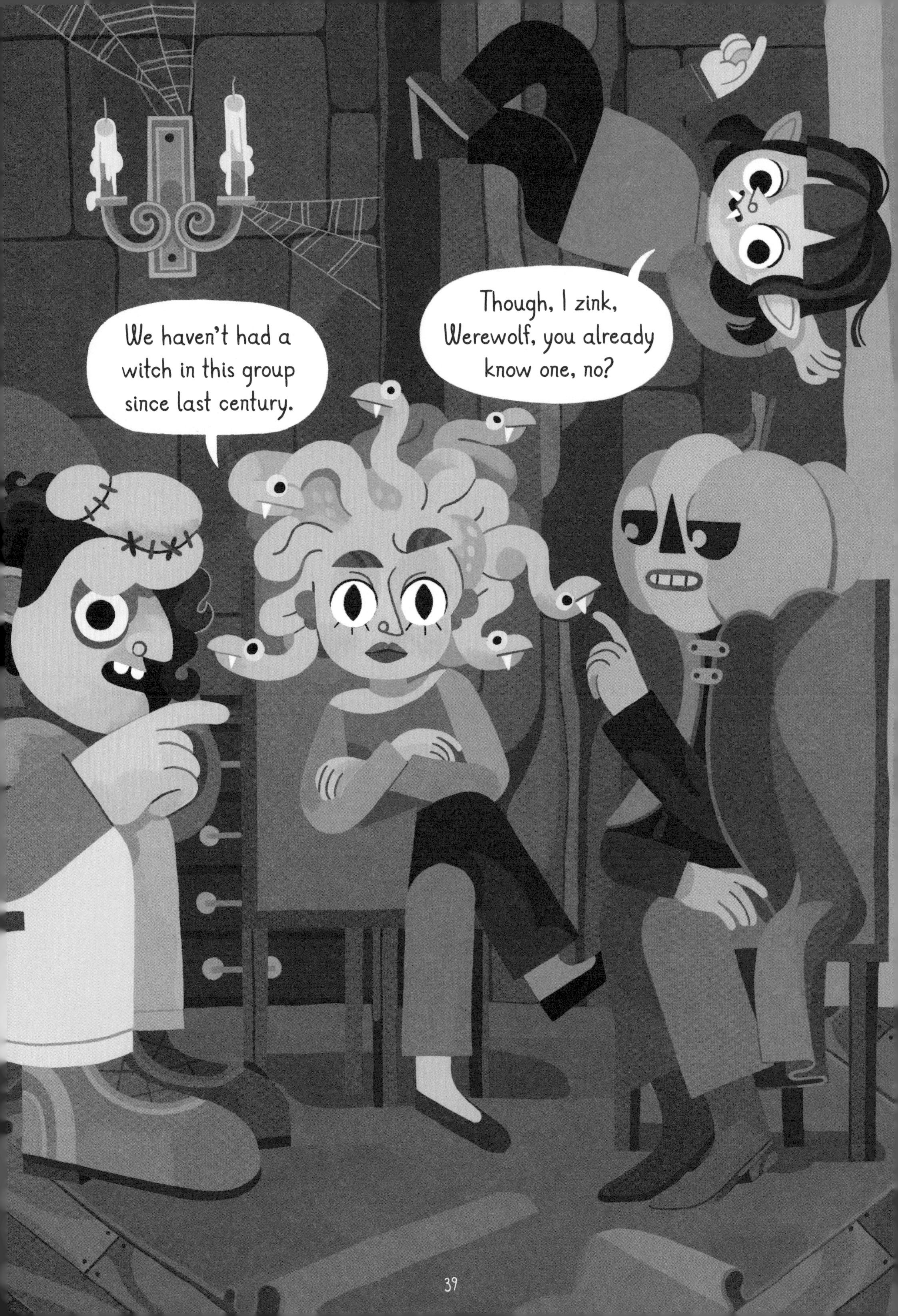
We haven't had a witch in this group since last century.
Though, I zink, Werewolf, you already know one, no?

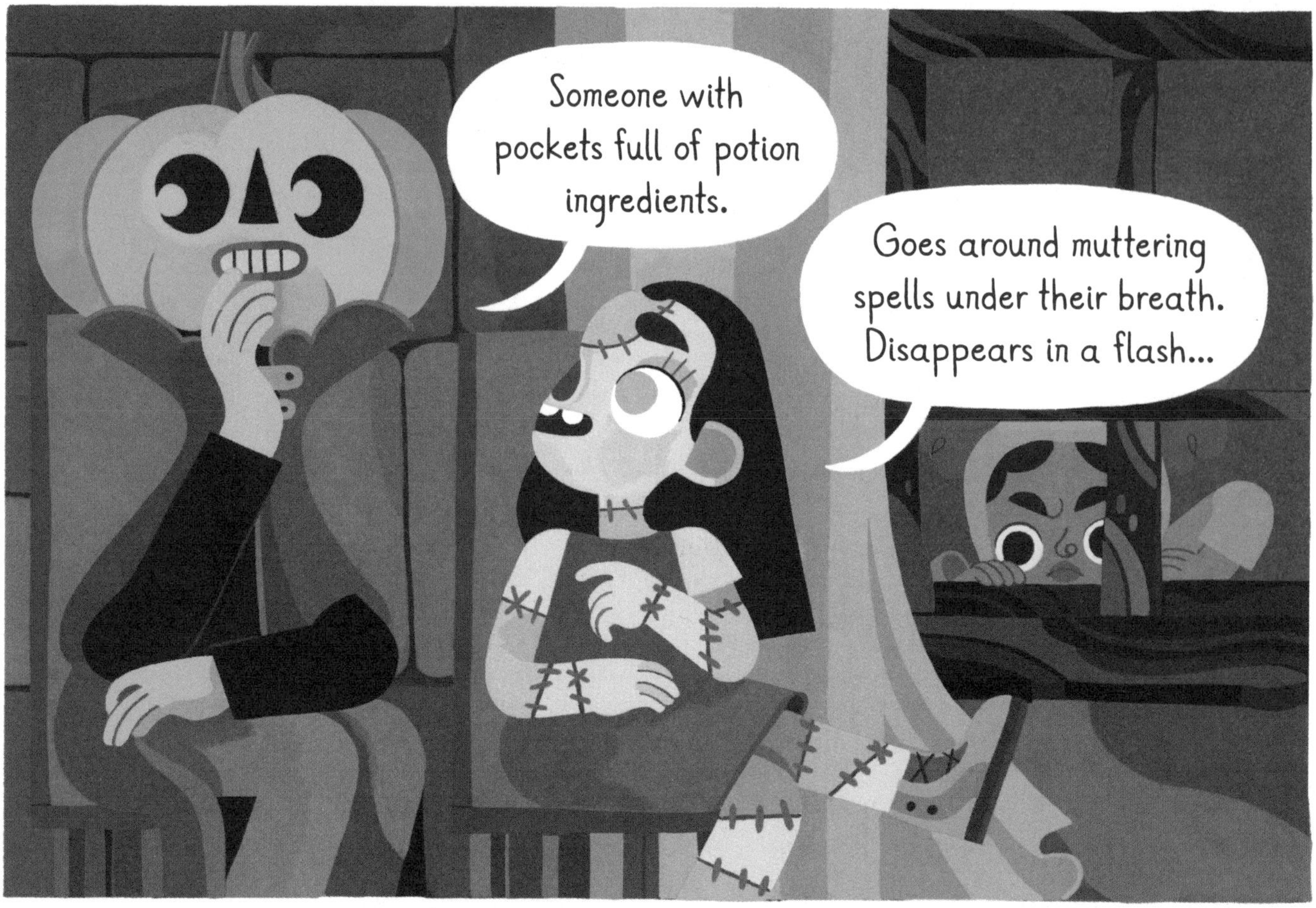
Someone with pockets full of potion ingredients.
Goes around muttering spells under their breath. Disappears in a flash...

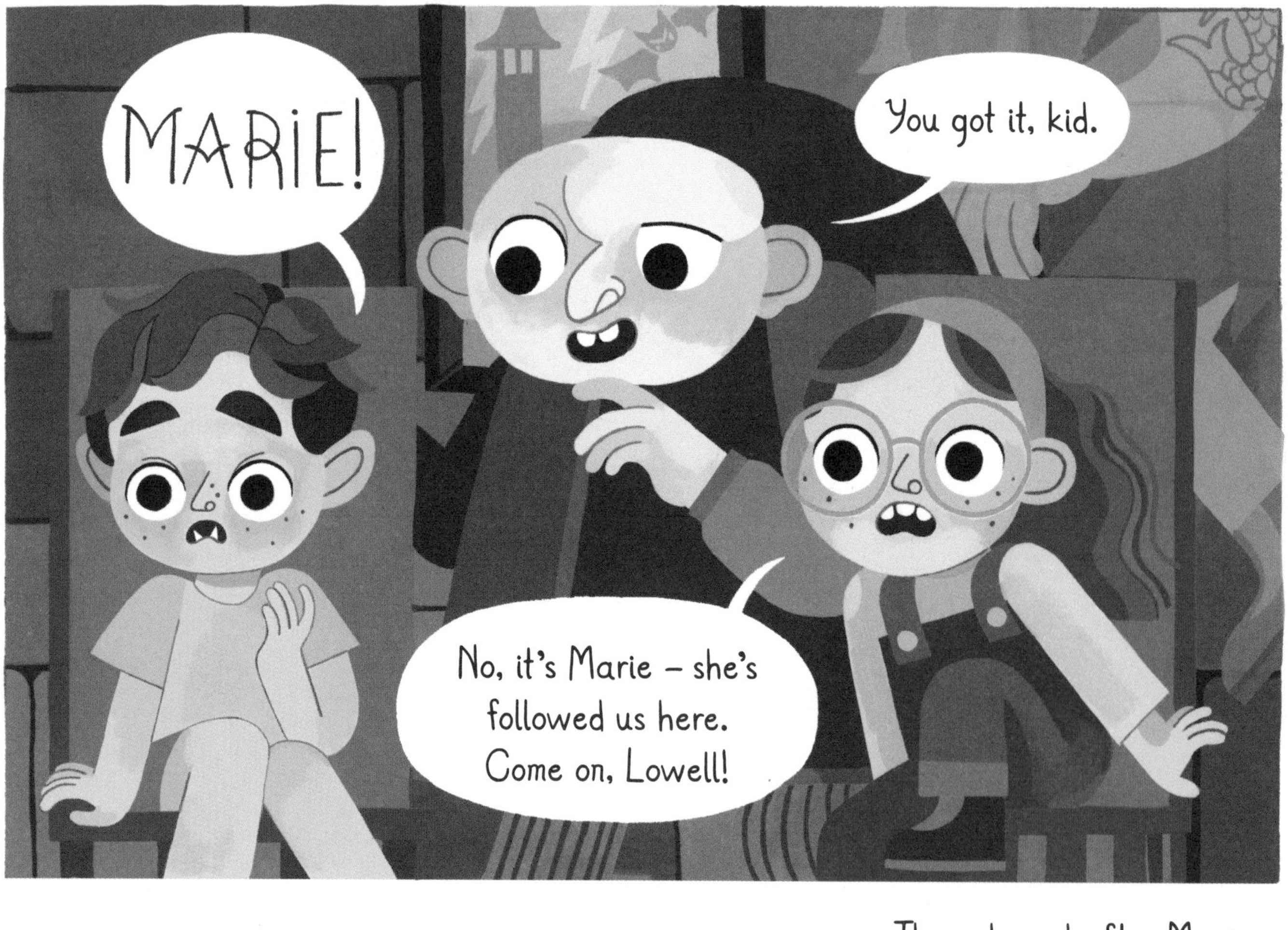
MARIE!
You got it, kid.
No, it's Marie – she's followed us here. Come on, Lowell!

They chased after Marie.

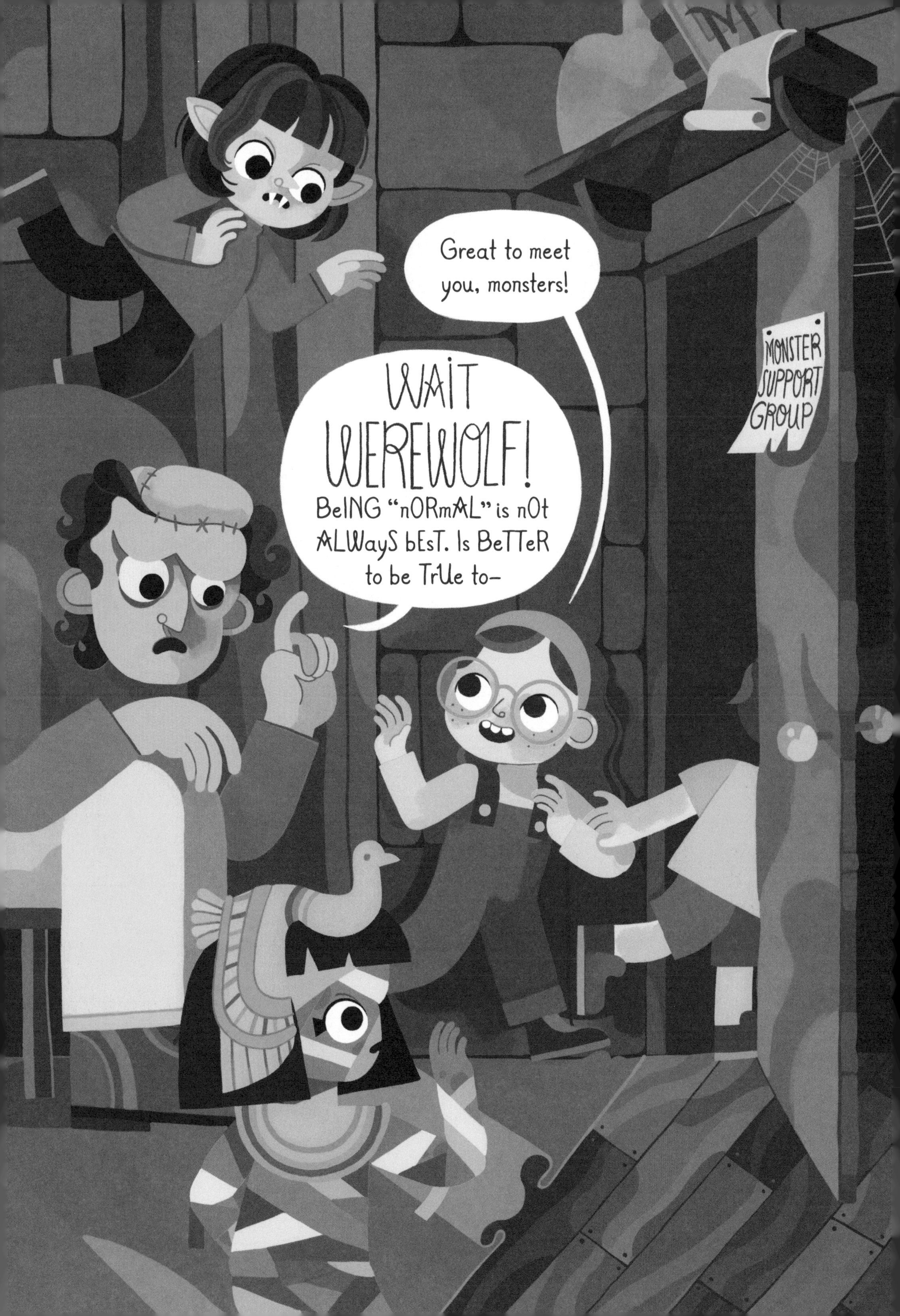

Great to meet you, monsters!
WAIT WEREWOLF! BeING "nORmAL" is nOt ALWayS bEsT. Is BeTTeR to be TrUe to–
MONSTER SUPPORT GROUP

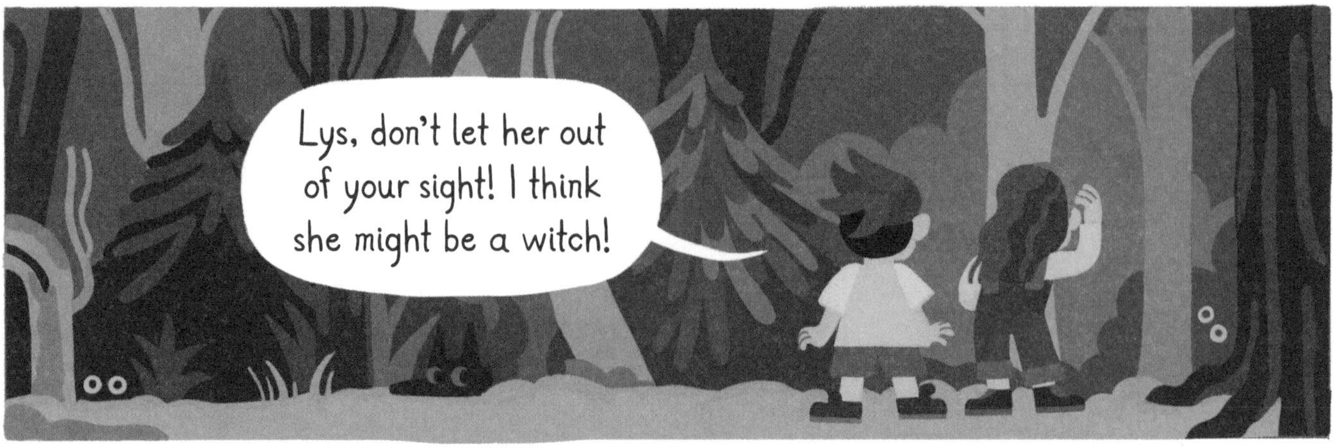
Lys, don't let her out of your sight! I think she might be a witch!

Lys and Lowell rushed out of the library. They chased Marie through the town, all the way to an ancient forest on its outskirts.

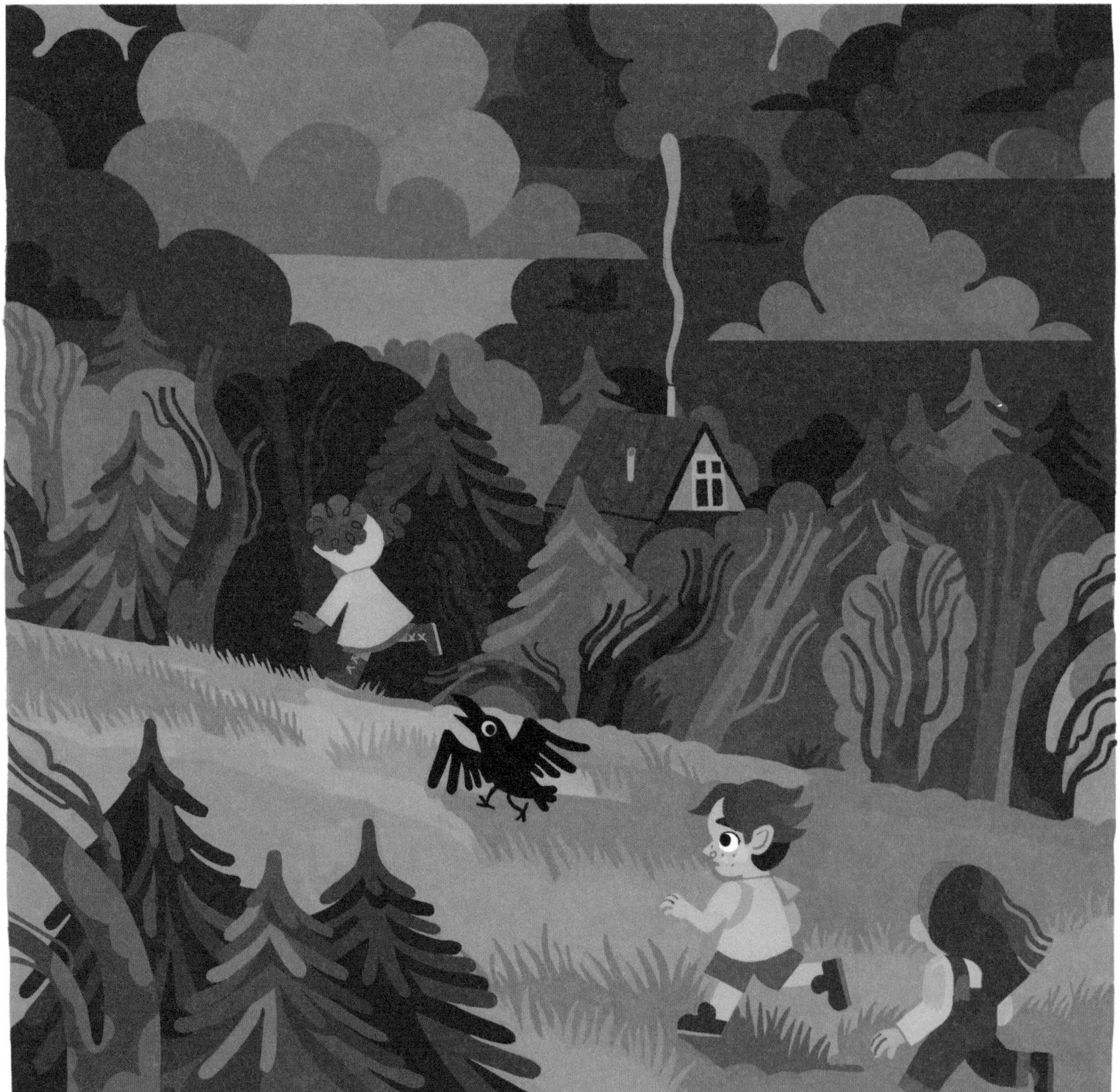

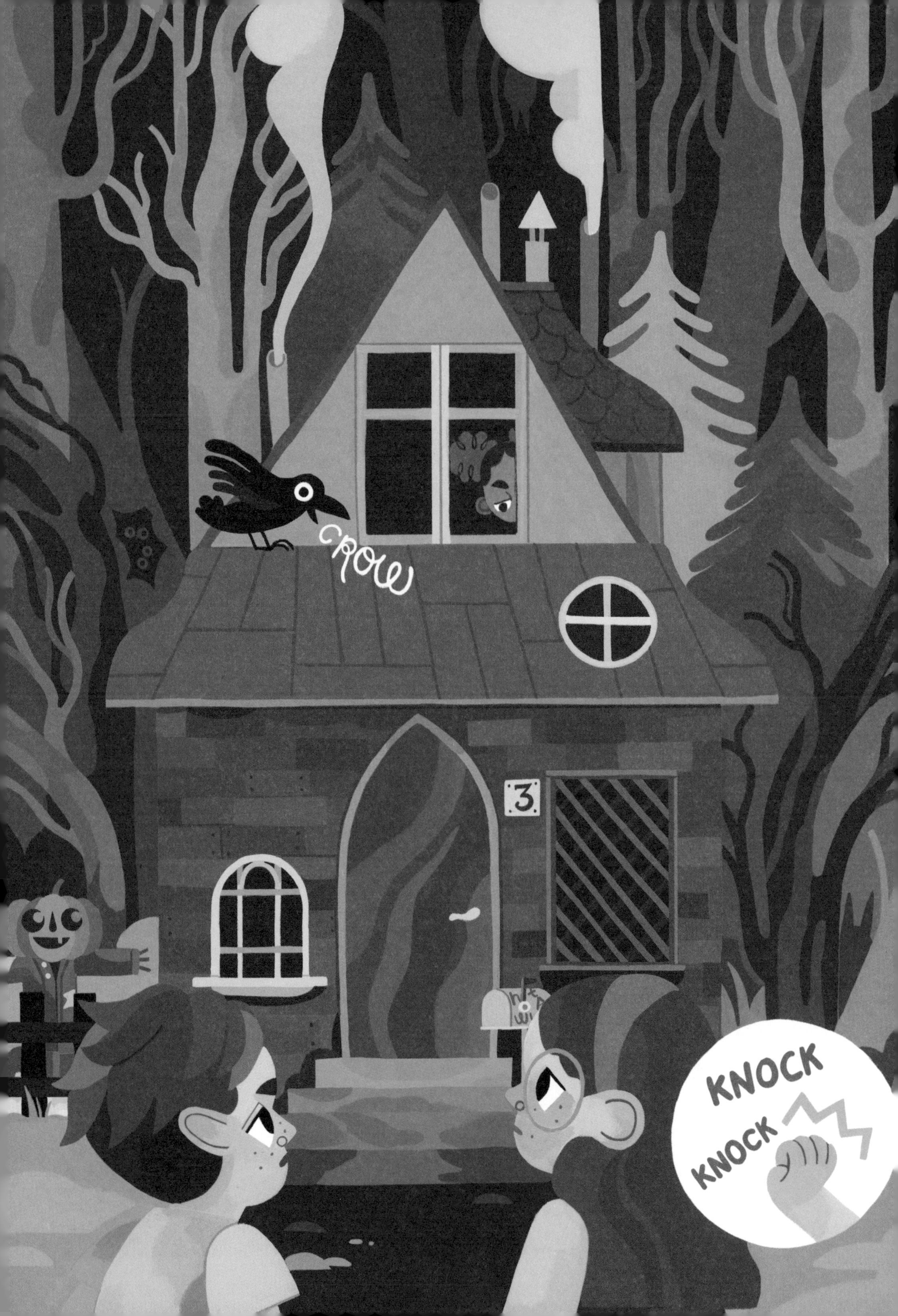
CROW
3
KNOCK
KNOCK

Lowell and Lys followed Marie inside her cottage.

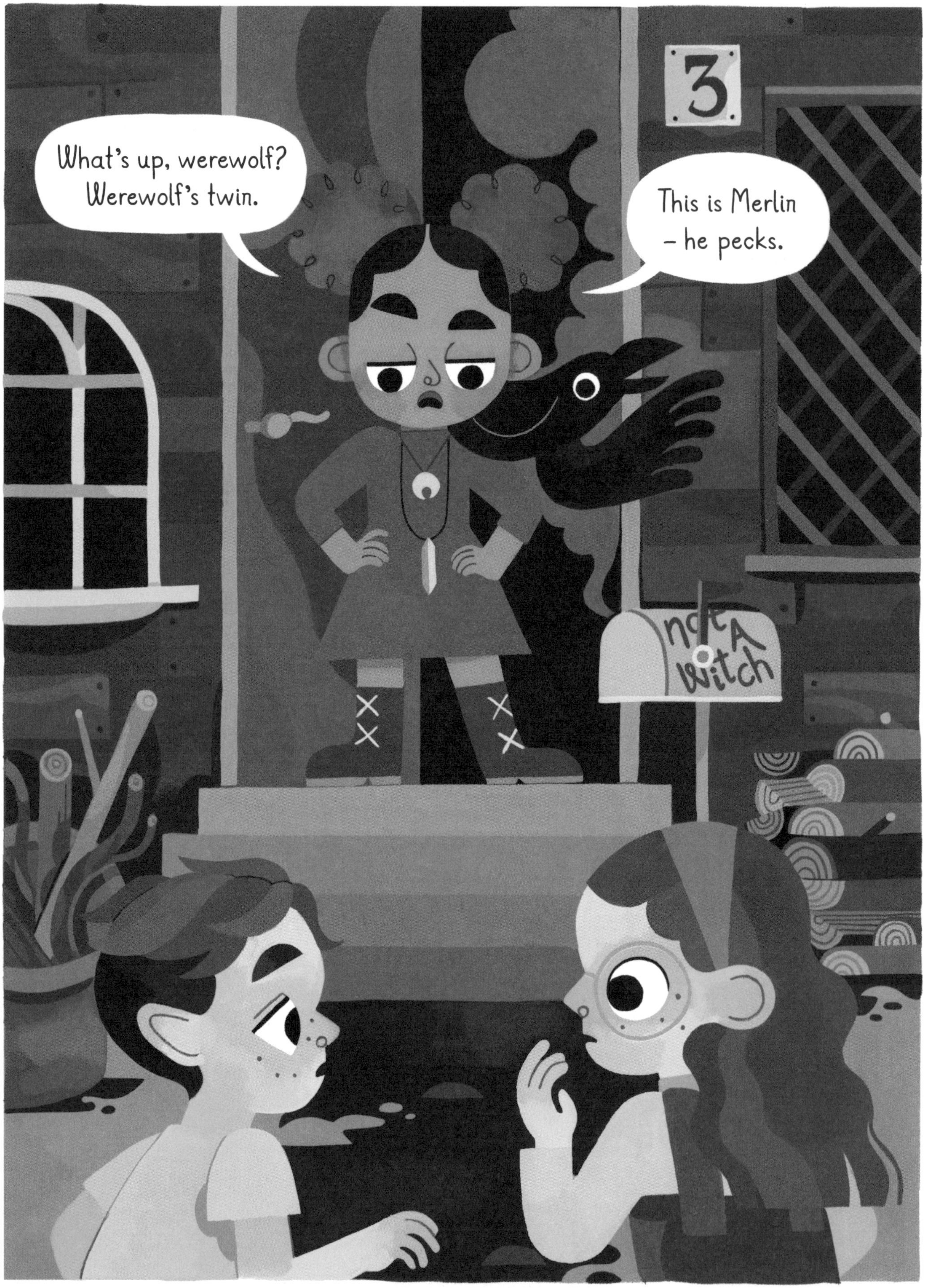
3
What's up, werewolf? Werewolf's twin.
This is Merlin – he pecks.
not A Witch

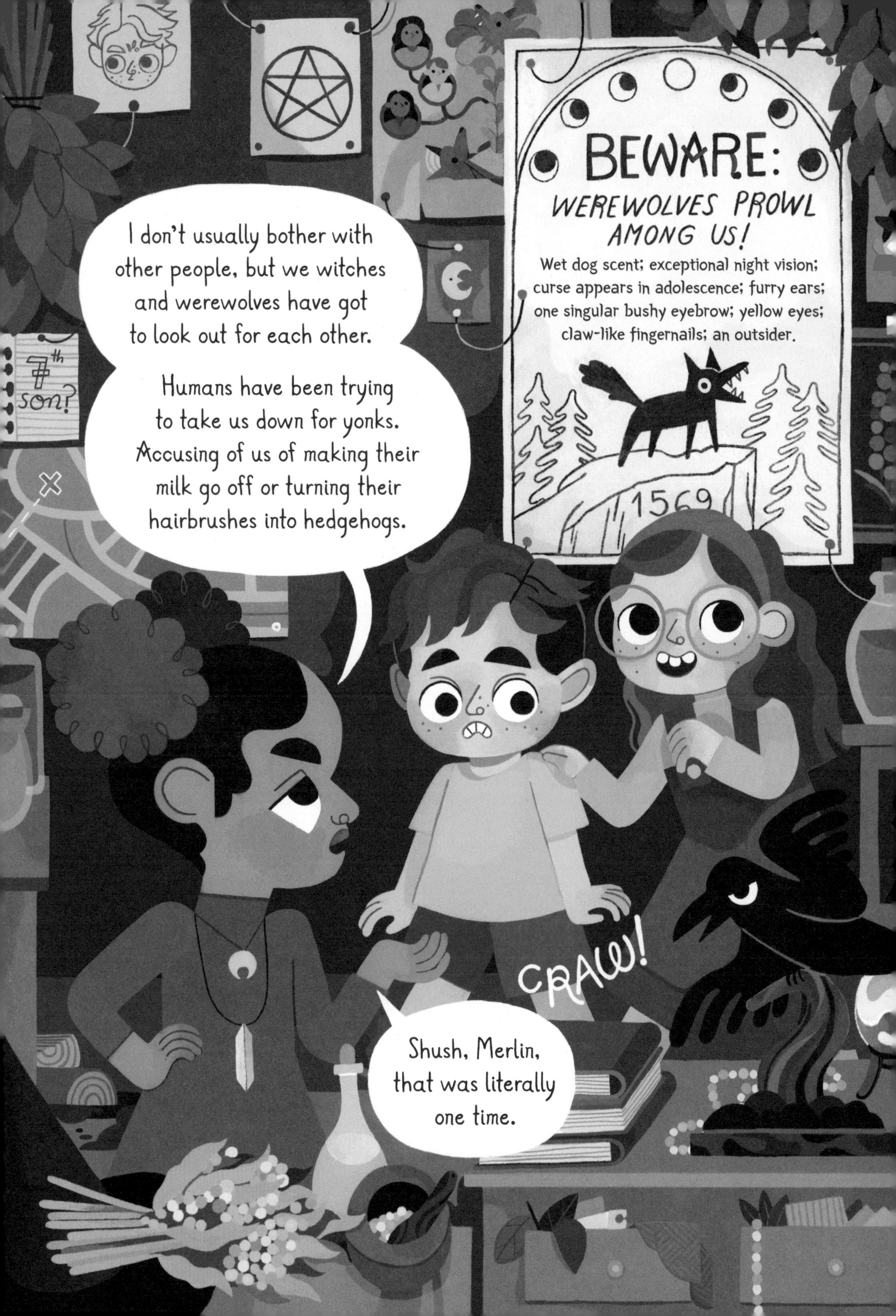
BEWARE:
WEREWOLVES PROWL AMONG US!
Wet dog scent; exceptional night vision; curse appears in adolescence; furry ears; one singular bushy eyebrow; yellow eyes; claw-like fingernails; an outsider.
1569
7th son?
I don't usually bother with other people, but we witches and werewolves have got to look out for each other.
Humans have been trying to take us down for yonks. Accusing of us of making their milk go off or turning their hairbrushes into hedgehogs.
CRAW!
Shush, Merlin, that was literally one time.

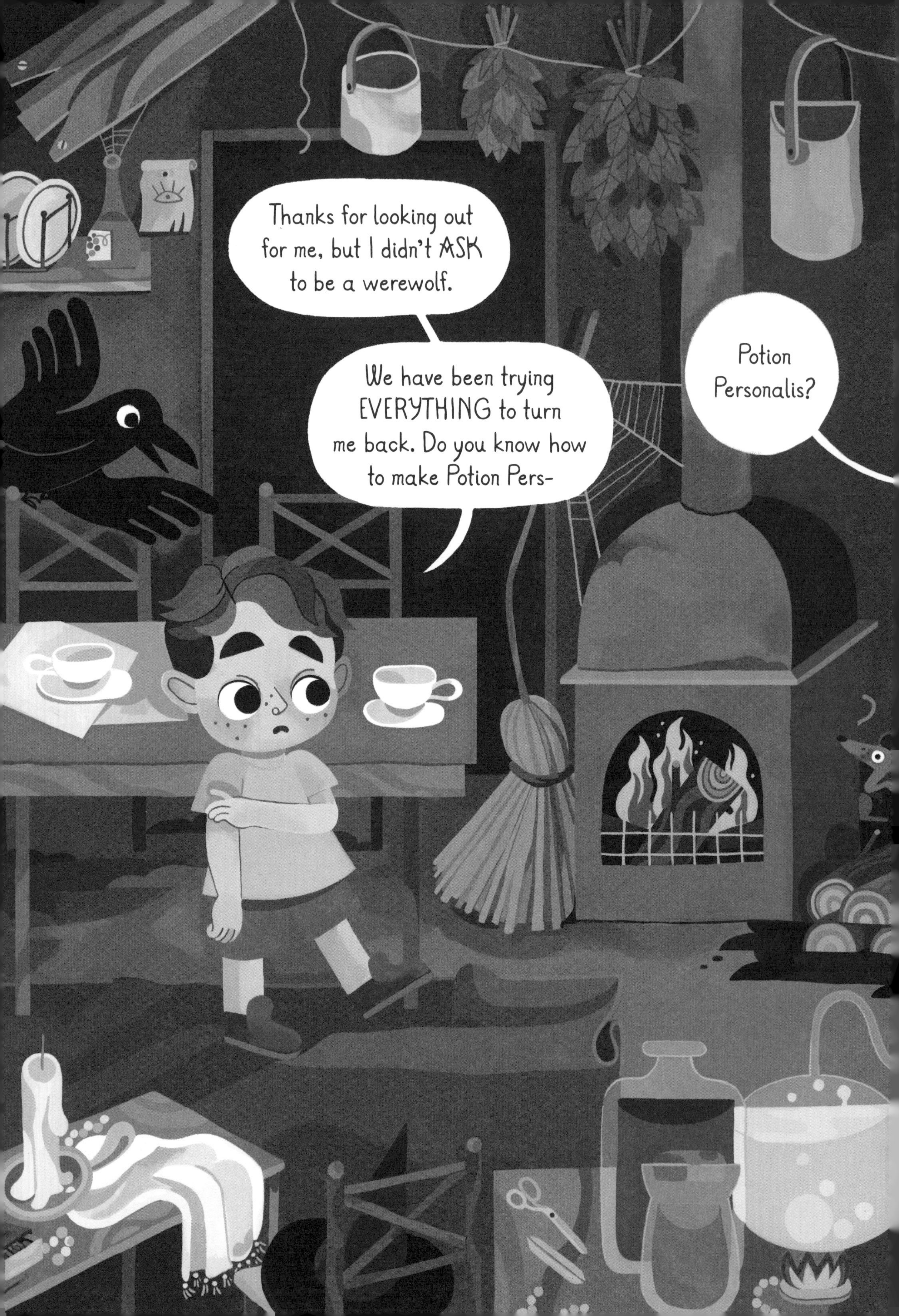

Thanks for looking out for me, but I didn't ASK to be a werewolf.
We have been trying EVERYTHING to turn me back. Do you know how to make Potion Pers-
Potion Personalis?

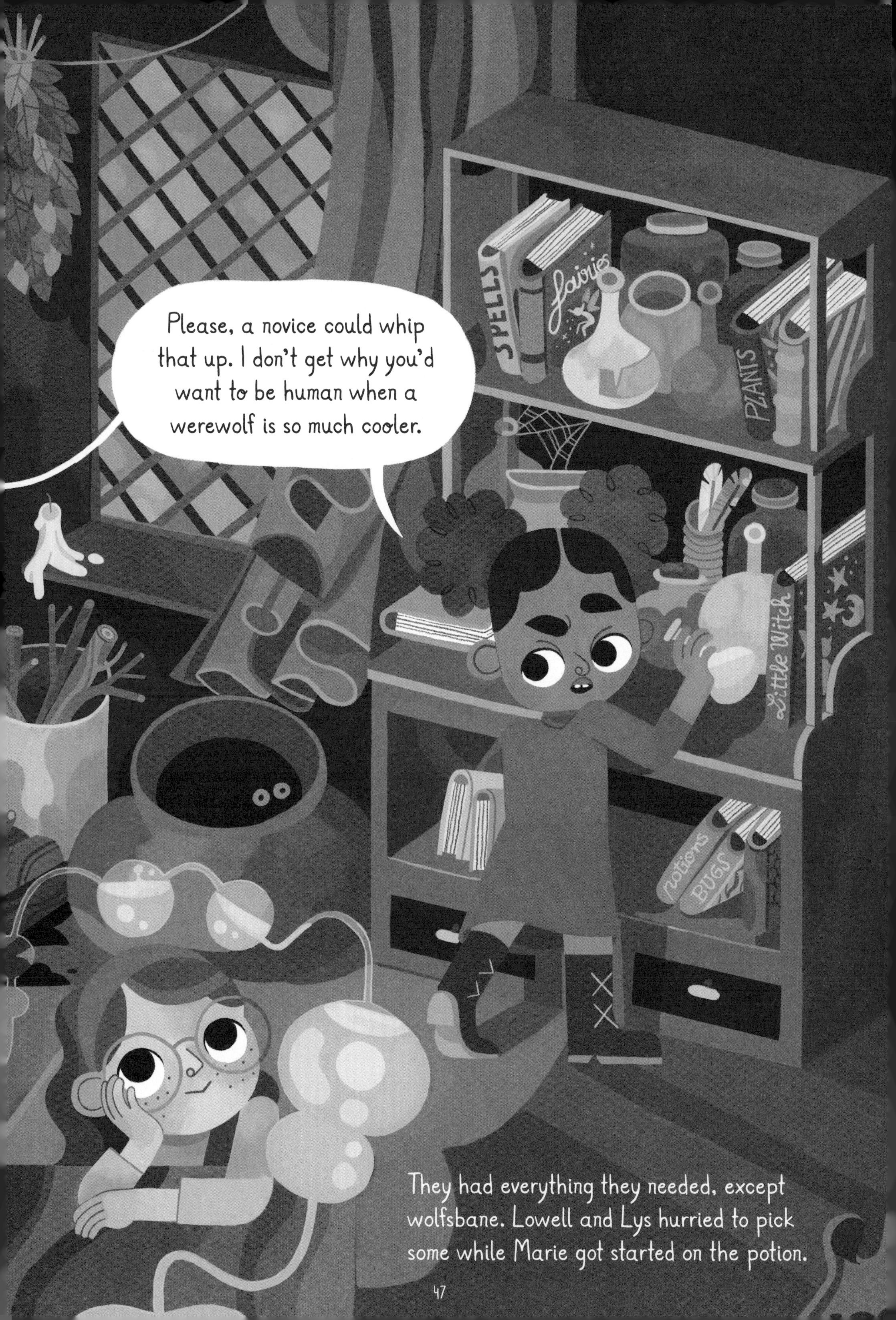
Please, a novice could whip that up. I don't get why you'd want to be human when a werewolf is so much cooler.
SPELLS
fairies
PLANTS
Little Witch
notions
BUGS

They had everything they needed, except wolfsbane. Lowell and Lys hurried to pick some while Marie got started on the potion.

Lys and Lowell followed Marie's directions to a clearing, where a plant with purple flowers sprouted.

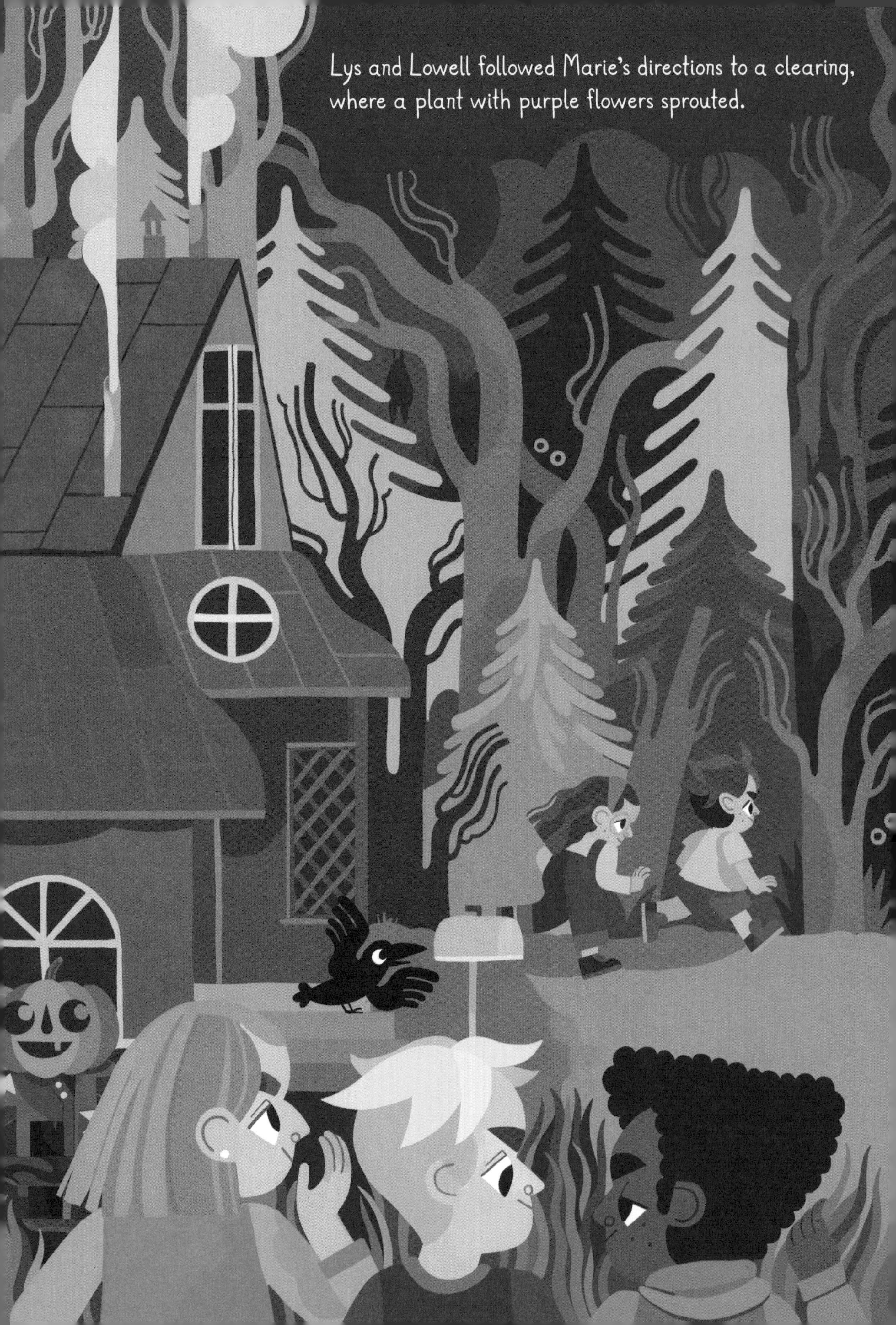

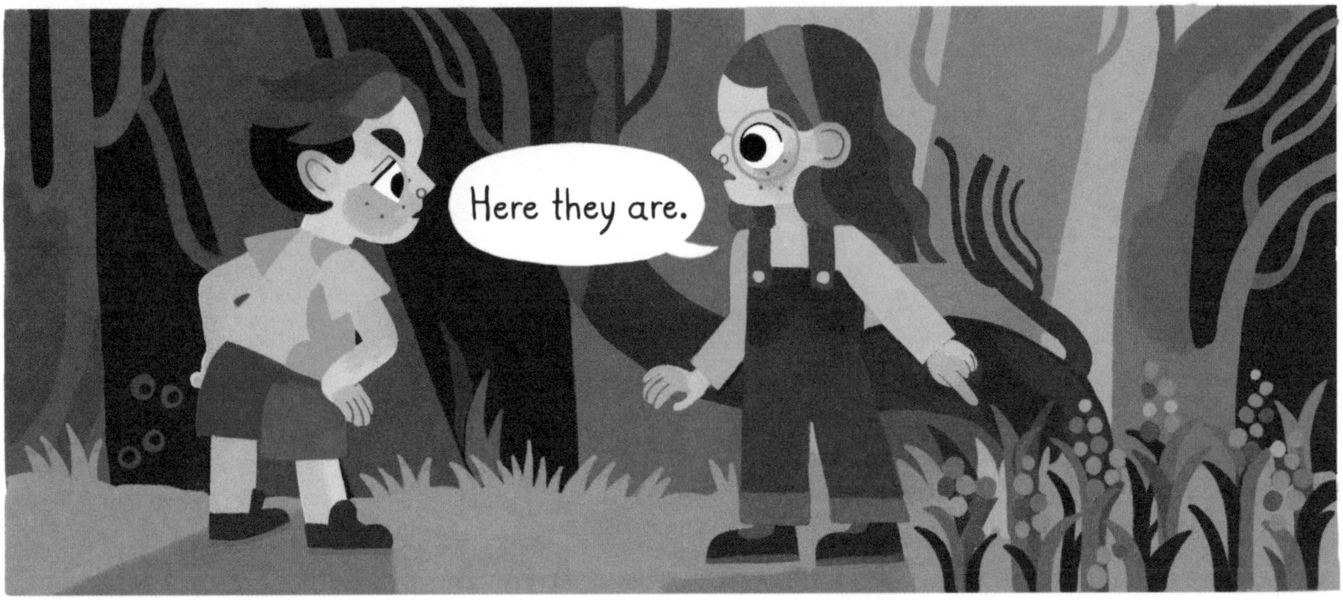
Here they are.

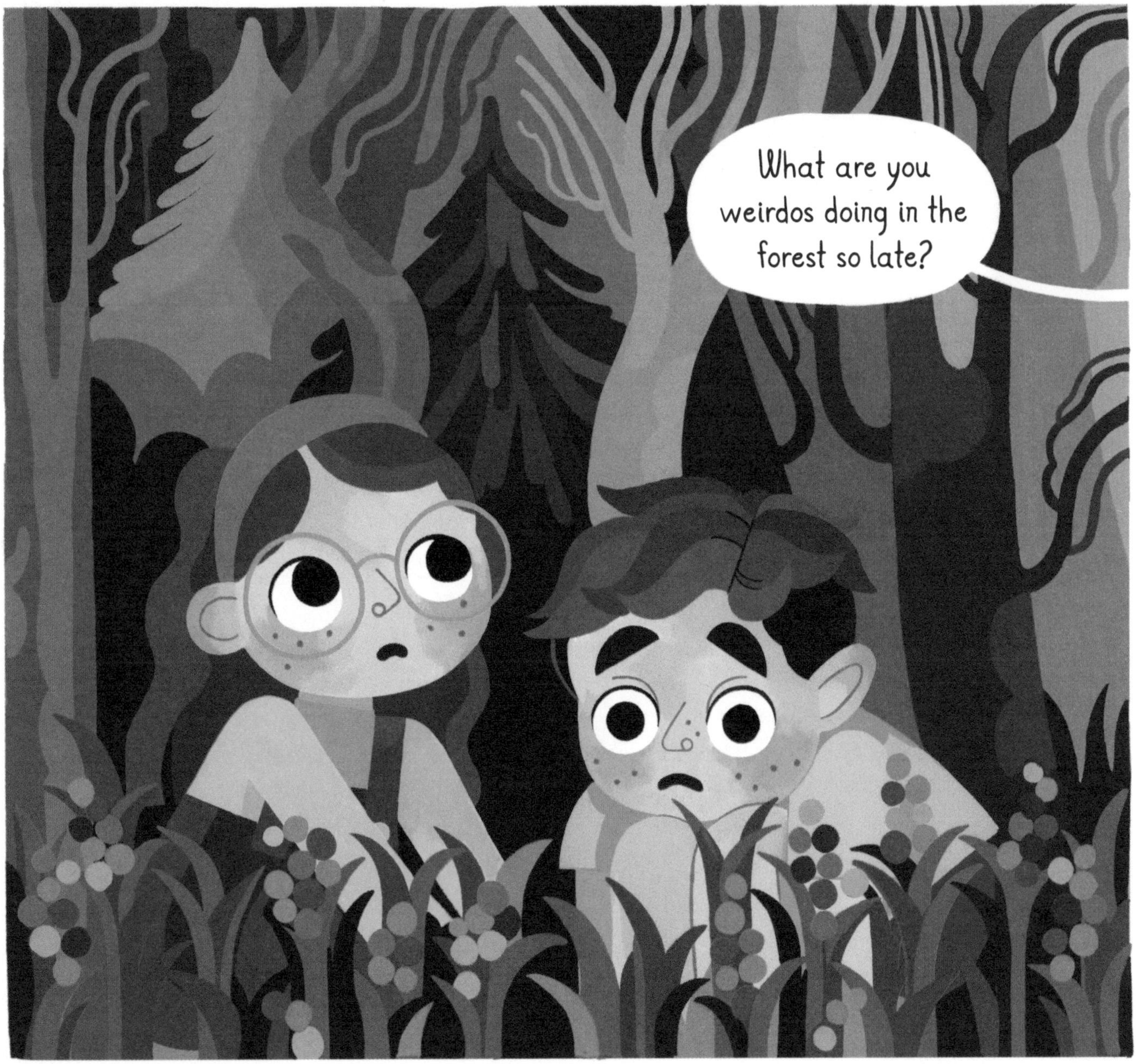
What are you weirdos doing in the forest so late?

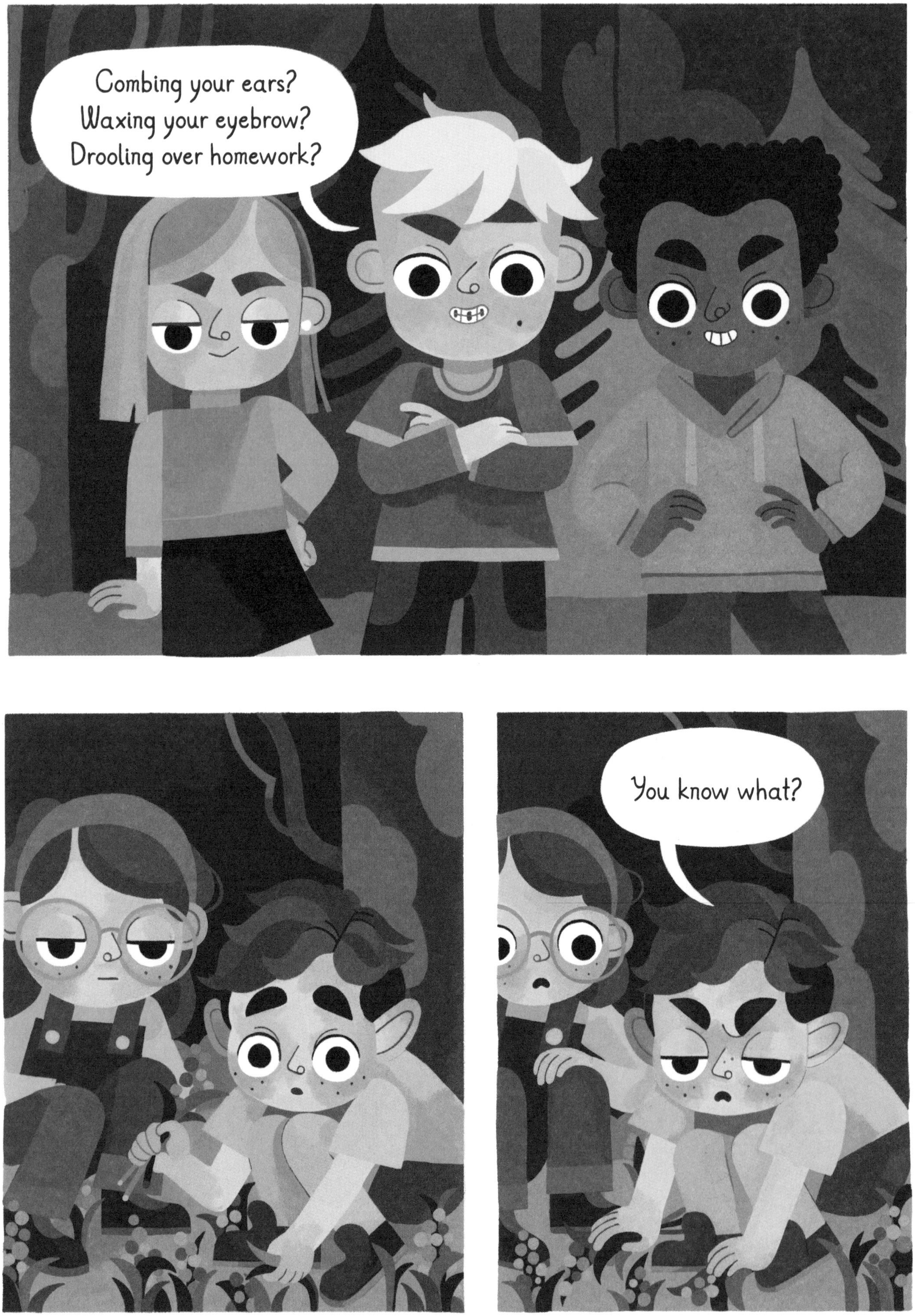
Combing your ears?
Waxing your eyebrow?
Drooling over homework?
You know what?

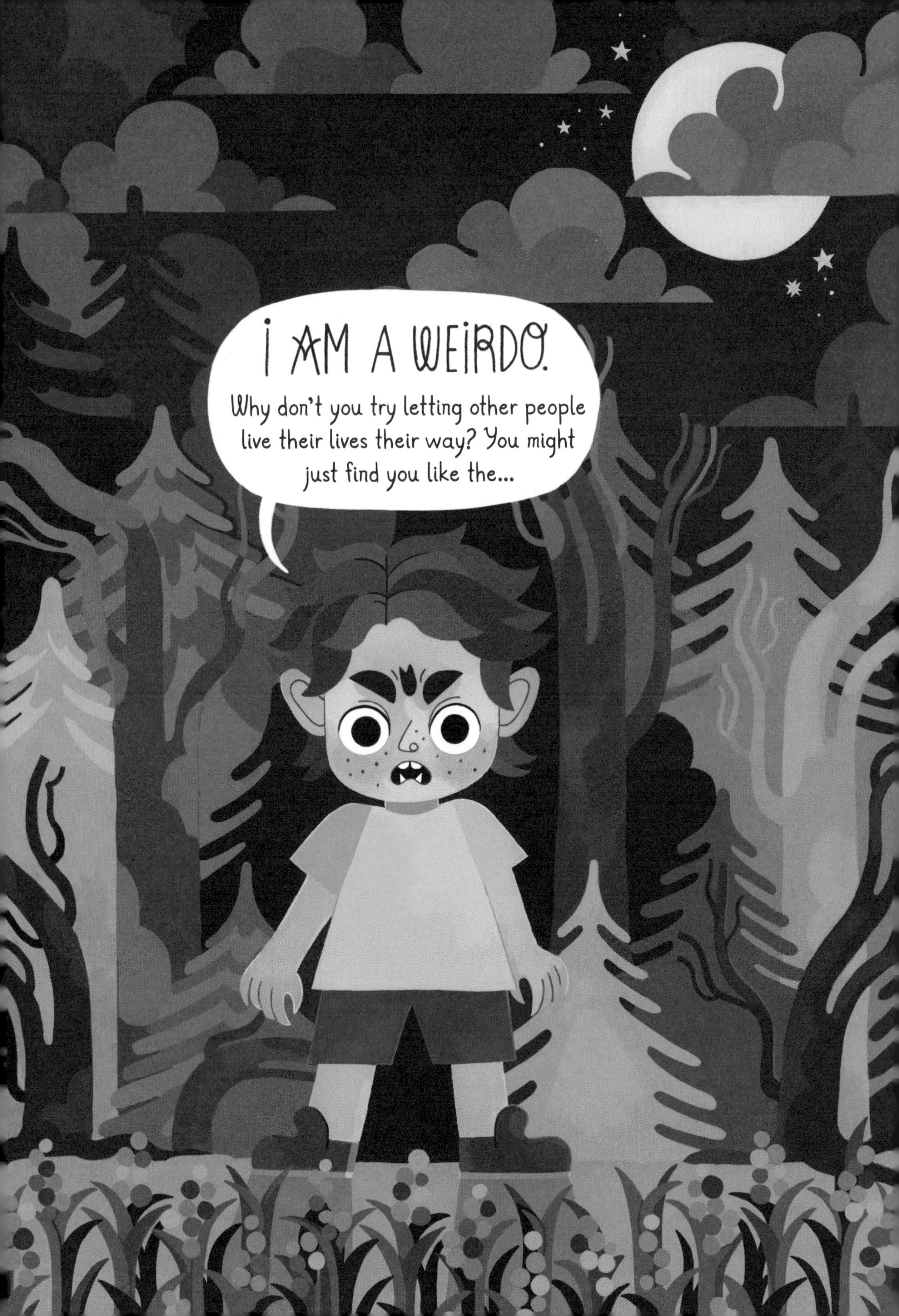
I AM A WEIRDO.
Why don't you try letting other people live their lives their way? You might just find you like the...

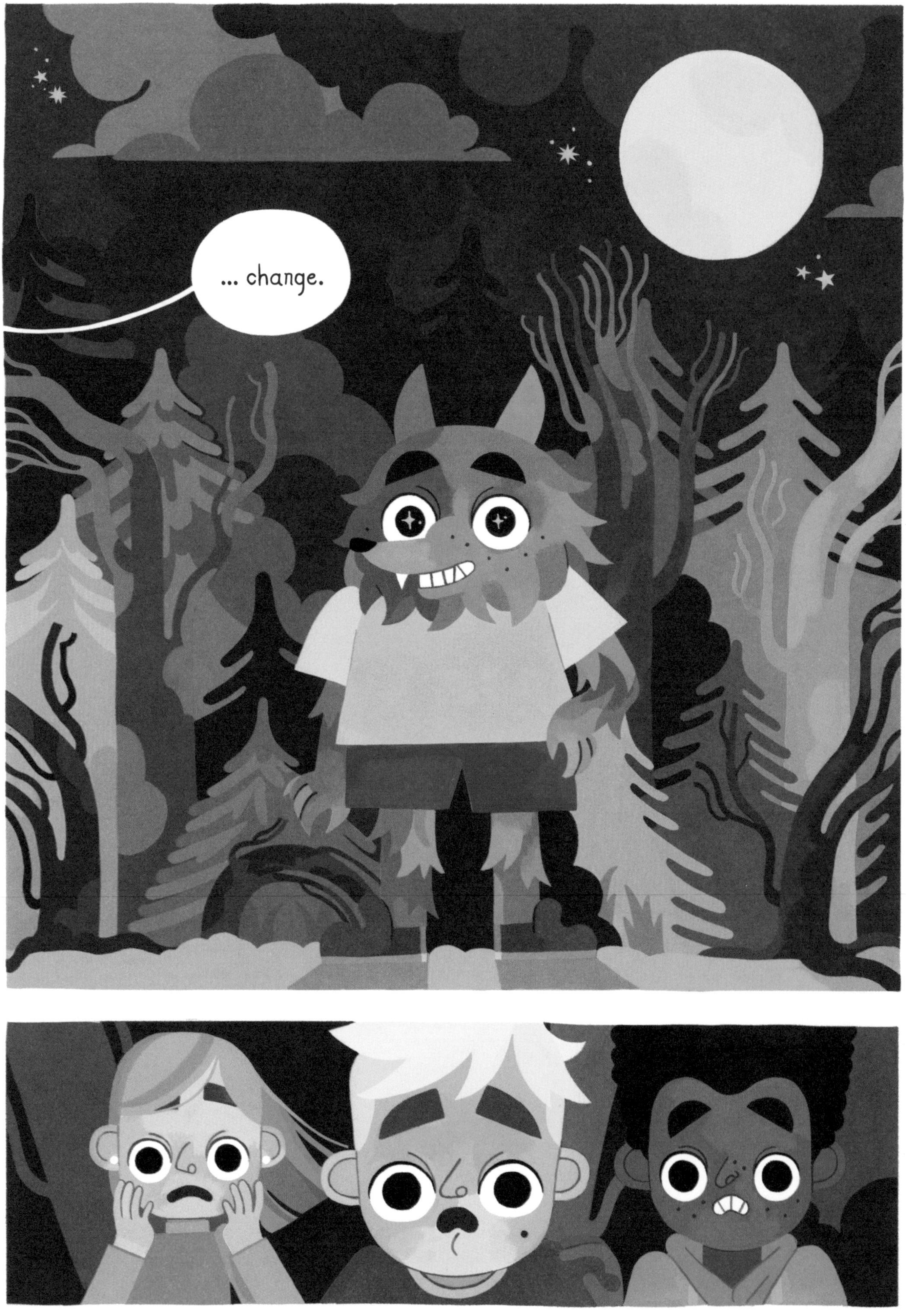
... change.

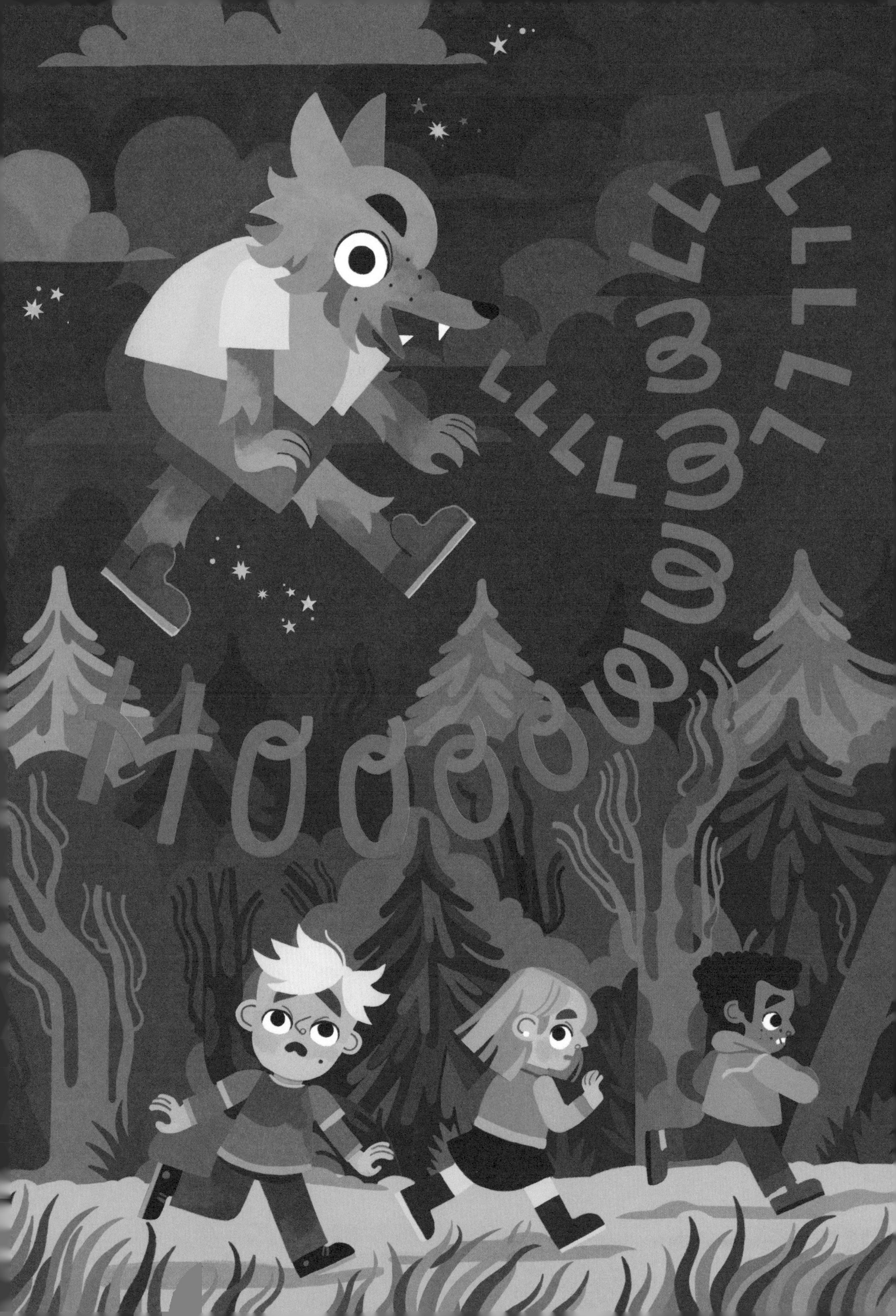
HOOOOOWWWWLLLL

Marie added the wolfsbane and brought a small bottle of the potion over to Lowell.

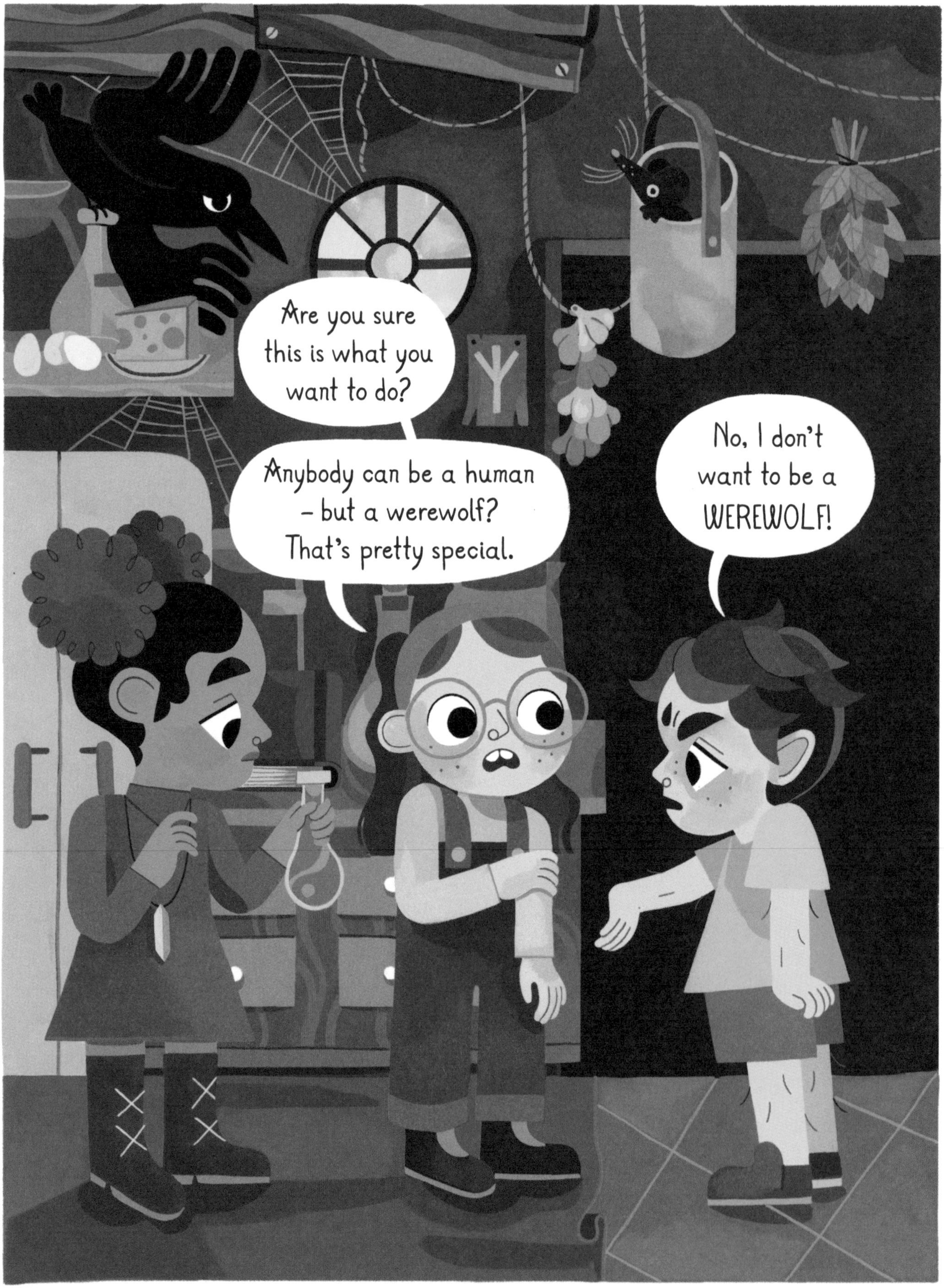

Are you sure this is what you want to do?
Anybody can be a human – but a werewolf? That's pretty special.
No, I don't want to be a WEREWOLF!

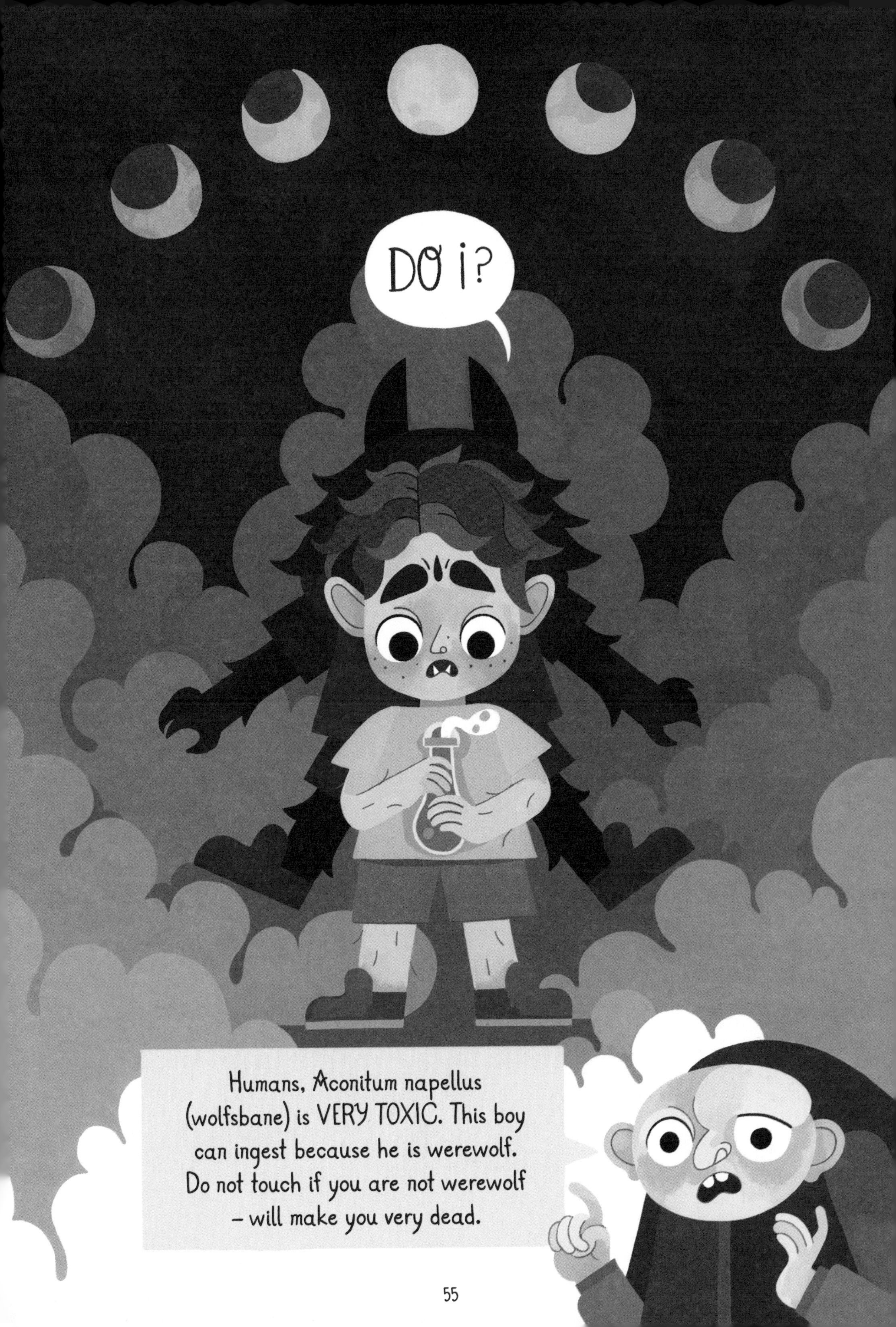
DO i?
Humans, Aconitum napellus (wolfsbane) is VERY TOXIC. This boy can ingest because he is werewolf. Do not touch if you are not werewolf – will make you very dead.

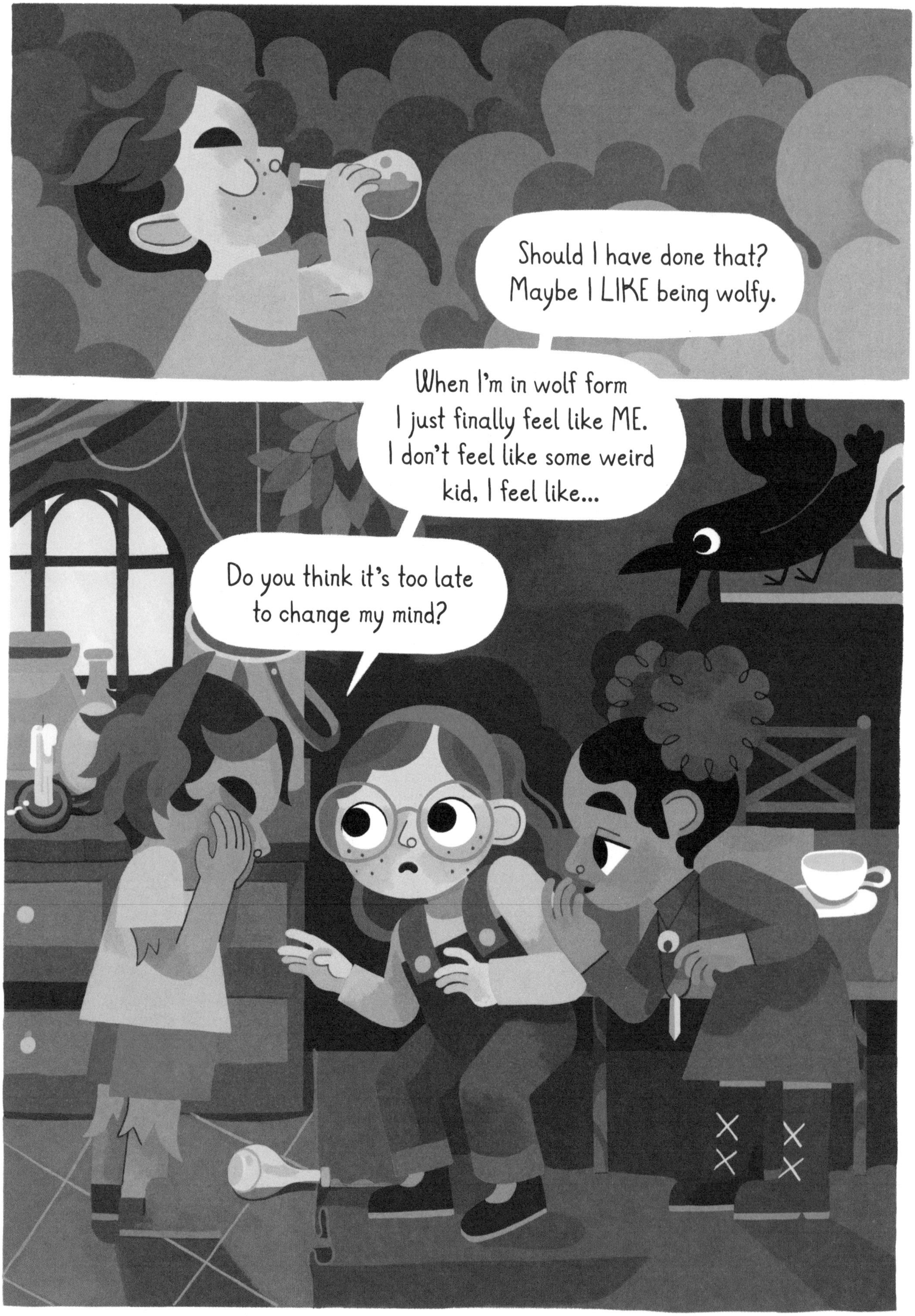
Should I have done that? Maybe I LIKE being wolfy.
When I'm in wolf form I just finally feel like ME. I don't feel like some weird kid, I feel like...
Do you think it's too late to change my mind?

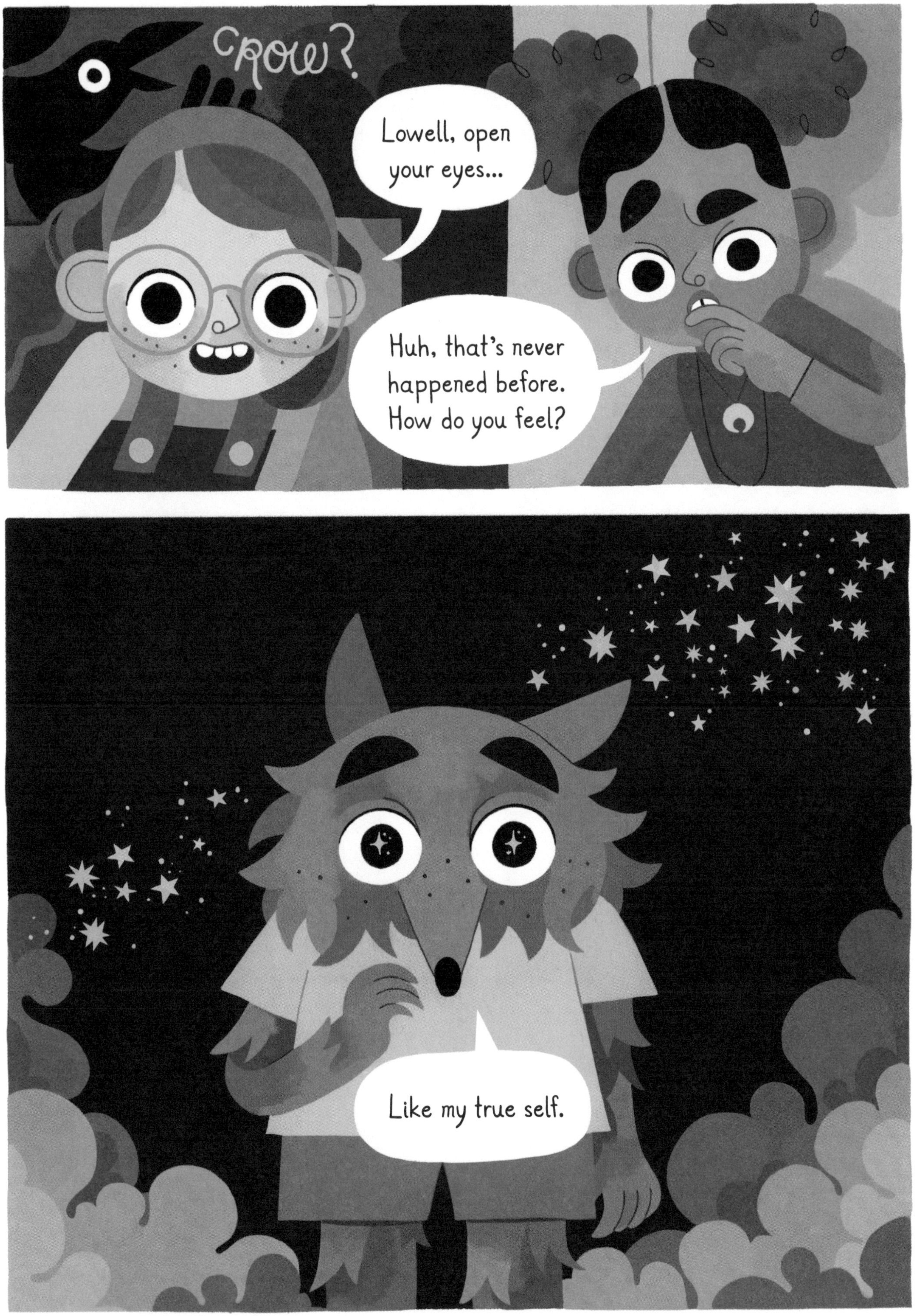
CROW?
Lowell, open your eyes...
Huh, that's never happened before. How do you feel?
Like my true self.

Lys and Lowell headed home as the sun rose.

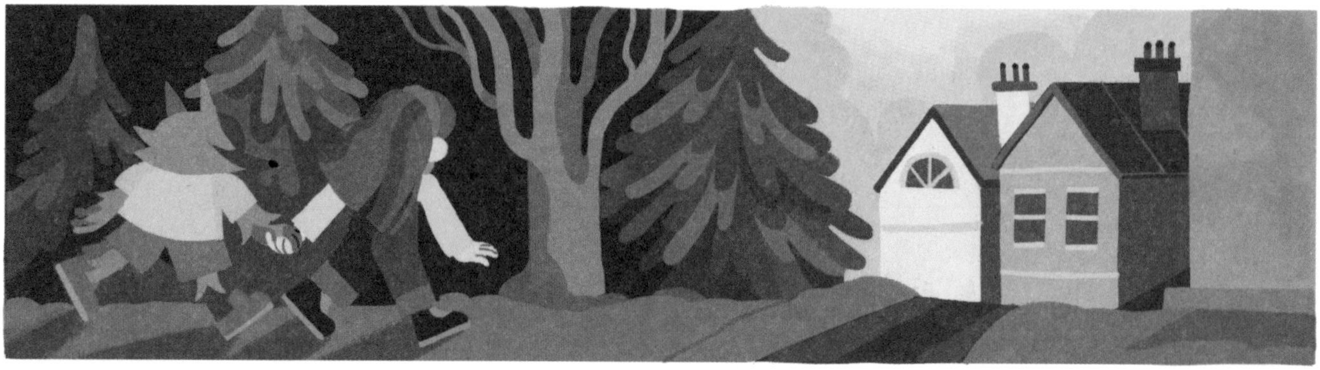

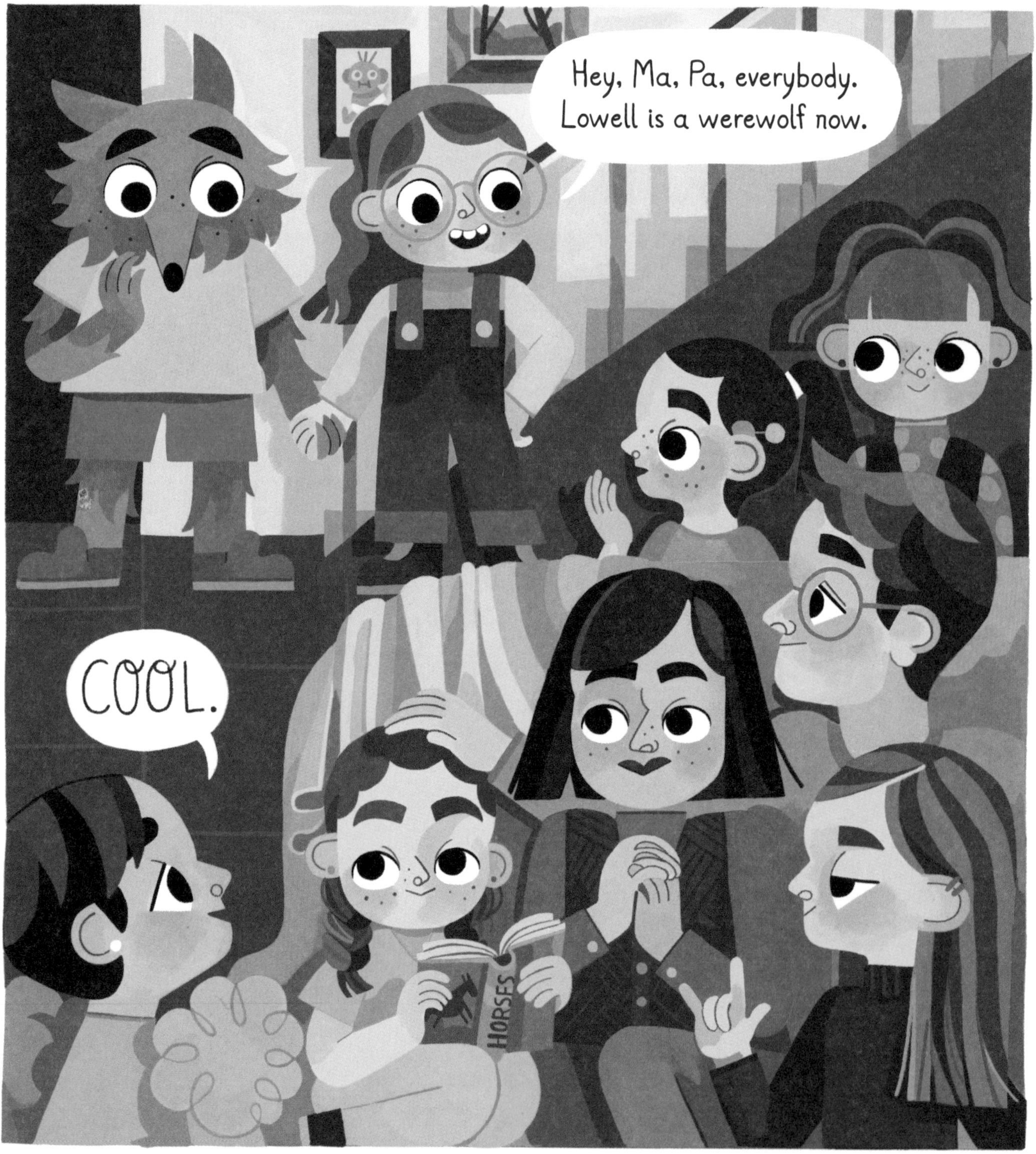
Hey, Ma, Pa, everybody. Lowell is a werewolf now.
COOL.
HORSES

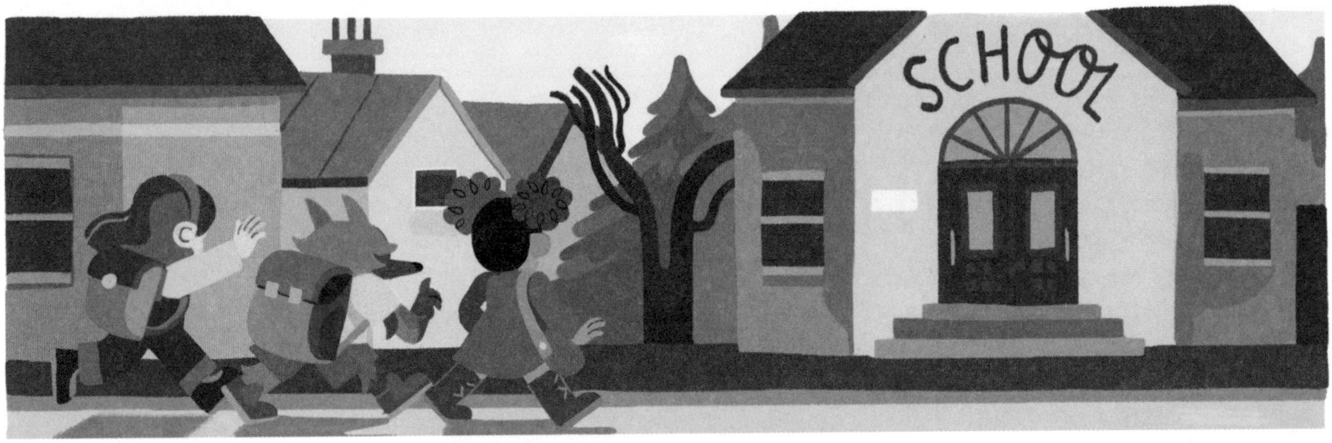
SCHOOL

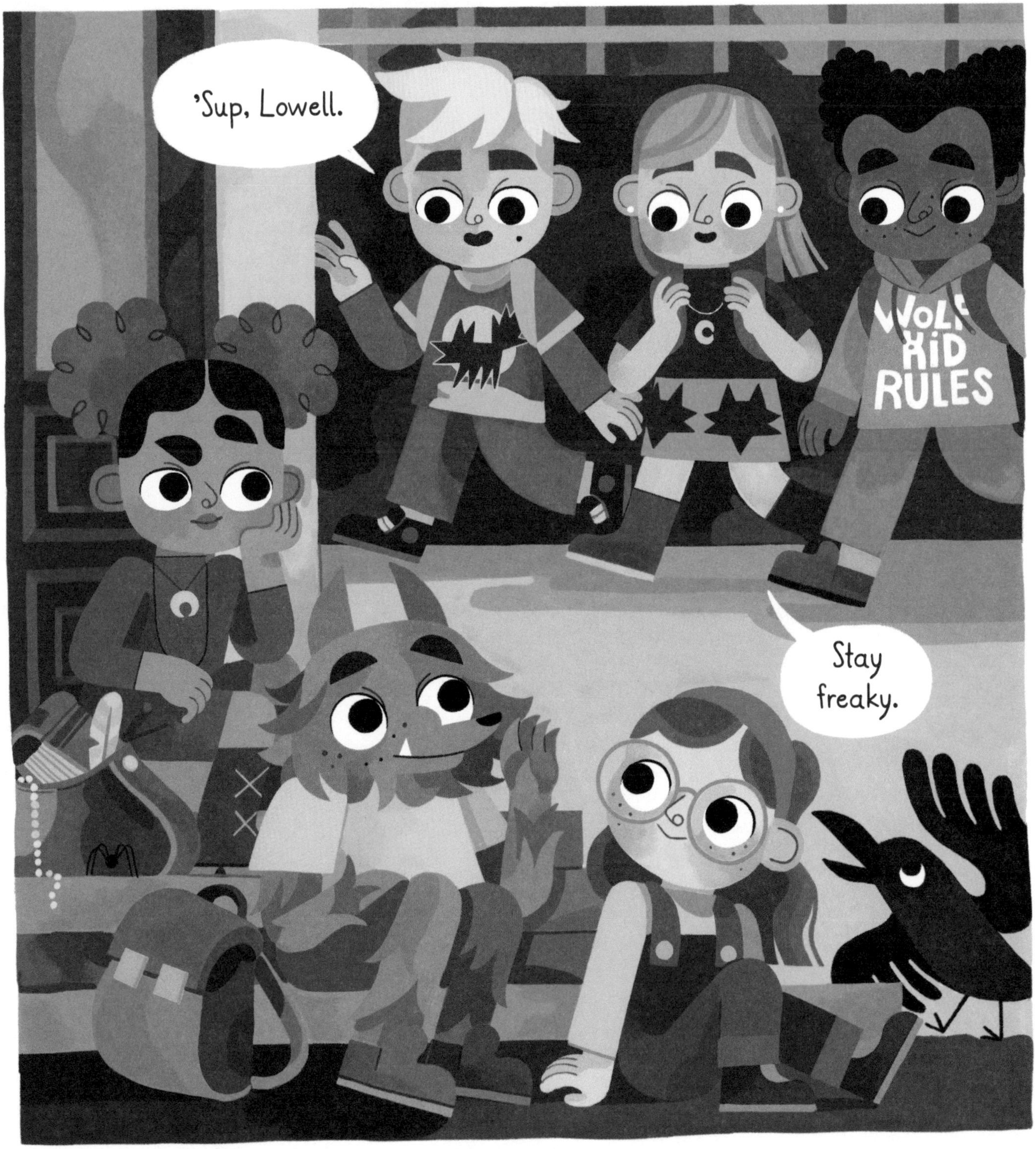
'Sup, Lowell.
WOLF KID RULES
Stay freaky.

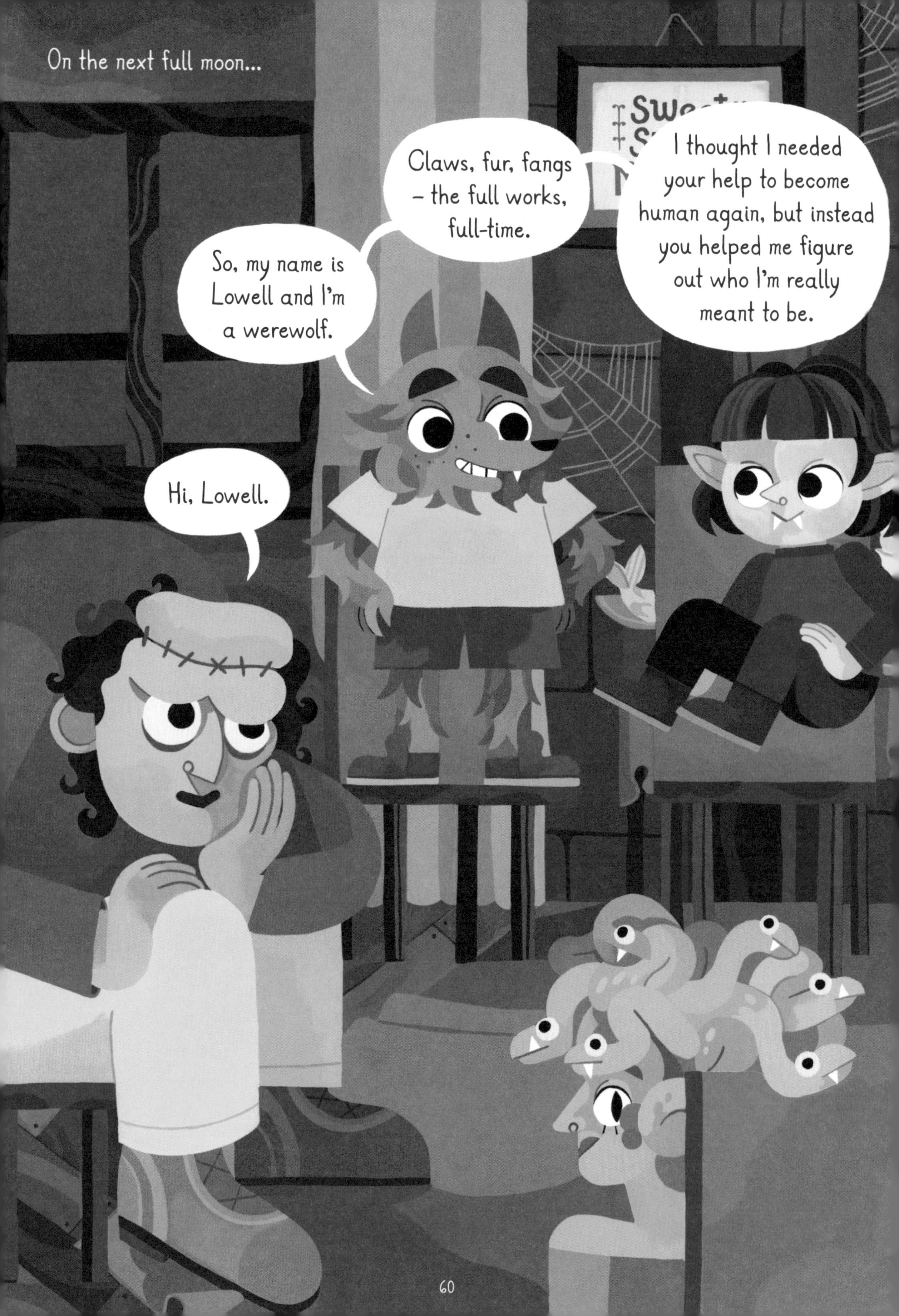
On the next full moon...
So, my name is Lowell and I'm a werewolf.
Claws, fur, fangs – the full works, full-time.
I thought I needed your help to become human again, but instead you helped me figure out who I'm really meant to be.
Hi, Lowell.

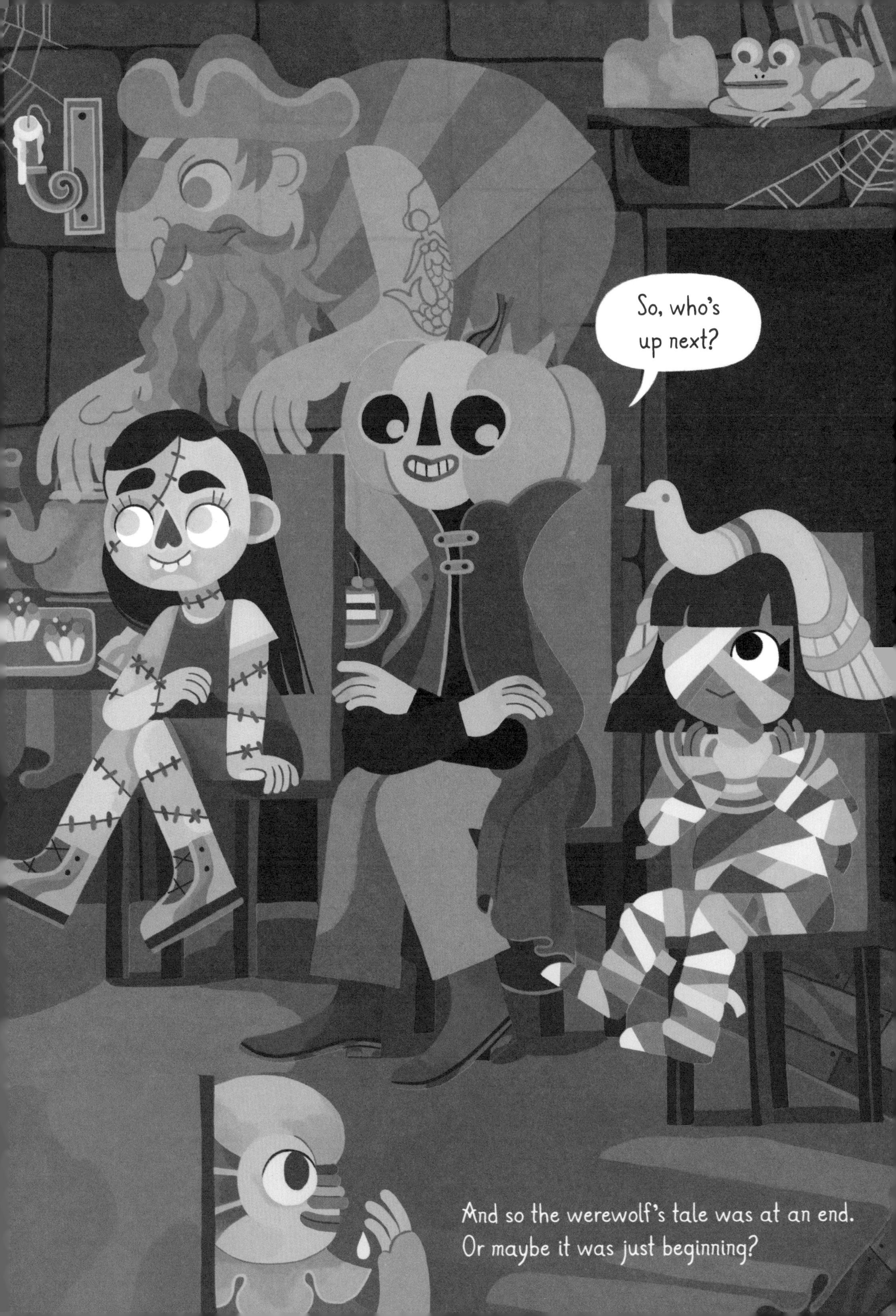
So, who's up next?

And so the werewolf's tale was at an end.
Or maybe it was just beginning?

LAURA SUAREZ is a freelance illustrator from Galicia. Since a young age, she has always been fascinated by books. She studied Fine Arts at the Polytechnic University of Valencia and completed a Comic and Illustration Masters in Barcelona.

Want to uncover more truths about your favourite monsters?

MONSTER SUPPORT GROUP: THE MUMMY'S CURSE

Coming Soon

Meet Anatiti: once chosen by the gods to rule ancient Egypt, this young pharaoh struggled to take help from her advisors. After all, she was the one chosen to rule, not them! But when tragedy strikes, and Anatiti realises she can't quite remember the path to the underworld, she is cursed as a mummy. Trapped inside a tomb for a millenia, found by an explorer and brought all the way back to the village of Dreadbury, this mummy still hasn't learnt how to take advice... until now.

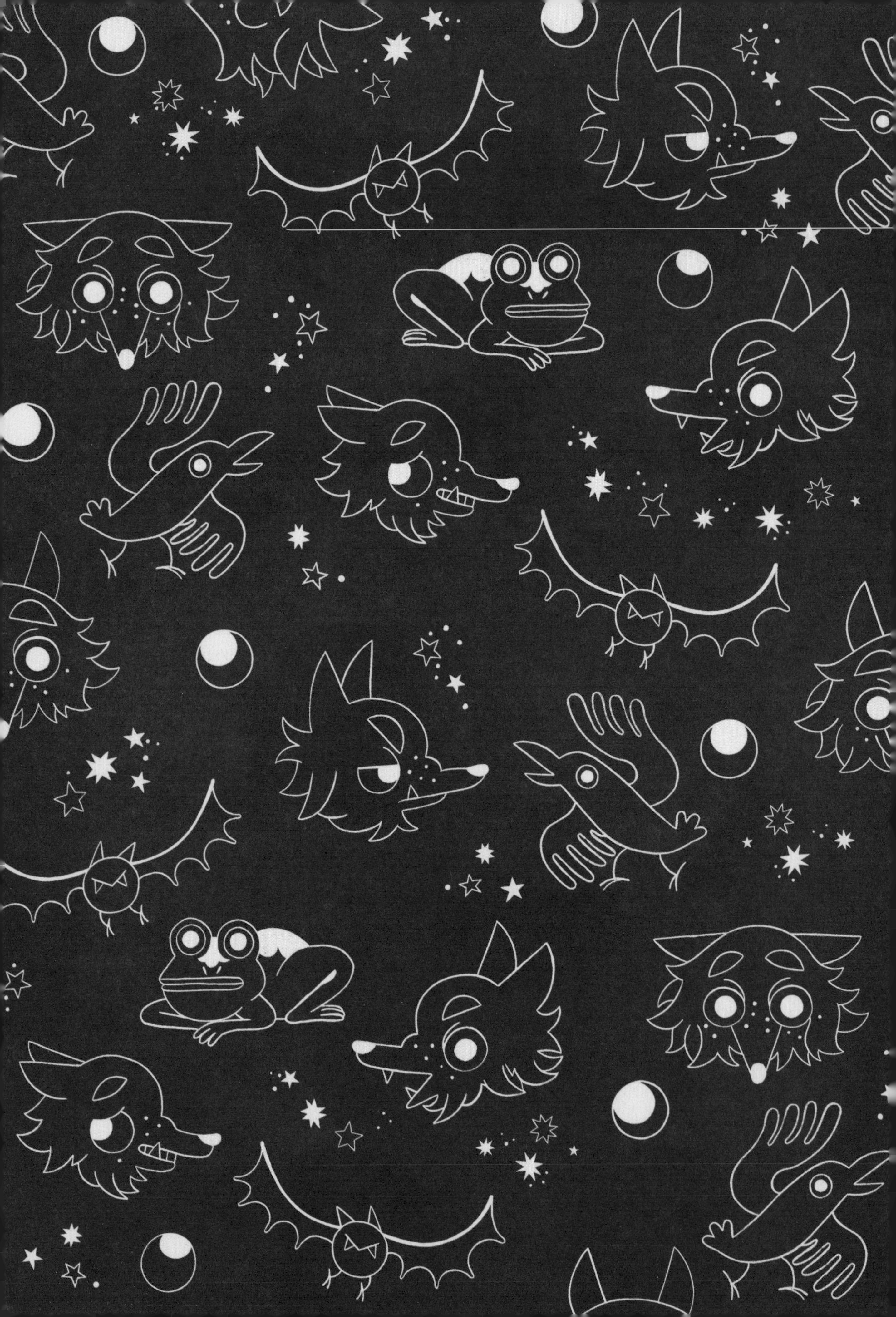